First Edition Paperback

ISBN 978-0-6456898-5-3

# WE USED TO

# HOLD

# HANDS

## ALL THE TIME

## NEPTUNE

## HENRIKSEN

# Content Notes

- Course language from the onset and throughout

- Non-linear storyline

- Allusions to, and mentions of, past verbal and physical abuse, by father toward children

- Allusions to, and mentions of, past verbal and physical abuse, by husband toward wife

- Depiction of past verbal and physical abuse, by father toward son, through fictionalised play

- Themes of past verbal and physical abuse, by husband toward wife, through fictionalised play

- Depiction of the moment a family is informed about the death of a family member, through fictionalised play

- Depiction of alcoholism and alcohol consumption, through fictionalised play

- Use of queerphobic language as a tool of familial abuse

- Background of, and brief allusions to, historical, political, and global events, between the years 1999 to 2023, both years inclusive

- One chapter mentioning a character's poor mental health during the 2020 lockdown

- Two depictions that may be distressing for those with claustrophobia

- Reclaimed use of queer language (including slurs) by queer characters, with some use during sexual and BDSM moments.

- Explicit sexual and BDSM content from the final third and onward, including degrading language and light bondage

*Also: This story DOES NOT employ the 'Bury Your Gays' trope.*

We Used To Hold Hands All The Time

# ARIA Top 100 Singles

# Year End Chart

# 1999

# No. 36

There he is. A kaleidoscope of regrets. A mirage of questions. A vision, of a memory, of a feeling, of an idea.

Like seeing the buds become poppies, and realising the time has been passing, the seasons changing, and the calm Spring has once again been engulfed by the Summer.

A new person. Renewed under the stage lights. Different now. And it looks good on him.

Like the tangerine and crimson that leaks into the leaves, finally giving way to Autumn.

Smiling. Teeth showing. So starkly different from when Jesse knew him.

Like reaching into the snow, and being surprised there's nothing in between the flakes, just fingers plunging into the soft freeze of Winter.

Matthew William Fletcher-Seng. Taking in his standing ovation.

And Jesse. One of the many standing.

Clapping hands to a static tingle, colour blushing into palms.

Vivid like the sun-glow of daffodils, opening with the Spring, against the lively grass, refreshed from its hibernation.

Jesse knows Matthew can't see him. And he doesn't want to be seen. Not yet.

Alone and bubbling with anticipation, trying his best to be patient as the theatre empties, and he hopes to come face to face, finally.

It's been an age, and yet a blink of an eye, but these last few moments, oh they are dragging, nails latching onto the dirt, grit gathering, pushing into tender flesh.

Muscles tensed. Pulse in the throat. Stomach in knots.

Shuffling, wanting with everything to push, to yell, to run and trample, anything to get to him sooner.

Useless jacket in his bronze fingers, scrunched under twitching fist, stonewashed denim between black nail polish. The extra layer unneeded in the November warmth, but Jesse brought it anyway, not knowing where the night would lead him. Or more truthfully, hoping it would lead him somewhere else.

Into darkness, through memory, under bed sheets, over to dawn. And it's always coldest in those small hours of city Spring. Especially when heading home after a hook-up.

Steps tiny. Seconds crawling. So many faces. But only one that Jesse wants to see.

And thankfully, muted light flooding in, the foyer in sight, the small brightness stinging, but maybe that's just the tears. Dried now, but these walnut eyes haven't forgotten.

Hanging back, trying to compose himself, Jesse leans against the poster-clad walls, eyes to the imperial red carpet, shoes passing, voices layering into a chorus. Plans being made, calling for drinks, sound-bite reviews, none of it any consequence for The Waiter.

And how he waits.

The crowd thinning around him, no longer wanting to skulk around the bar, shouts muting to indoor voices, no longer needing to cut through so many bodies, a balance gradually muting the chaos, no longer congested by the masses.

And he emerges. Finally.

Matthew.

Trepidatious. With hands clasped in front of his chest. Onyx eyes darting. Taller. Bigger. The same but incredibly changed.

He's snapped up immediately, seeming to know the one bold enough to be first, face lighting up as they squeeze his arm, nodding as they gesture heartedly, watching with intention as they introduce another.

Jesse watching. Taking Matthew in from afar.

Hair so much longer, still jet black and thick, dead straight, brushing his shoulders as he smiles and leans in, giving each person he's undivided attention.

Eyes brighter, irises still deep and dark, twinkling as he nods along, then looking to the ceiling's art deco lights, as he raises his hands in delight.

Skin glowing, carmine undertones peeking through almond warmth, the post-performance atmosphere electric, feeding energy into, and through, the buzzing beings huddling around him.

Chattering and praise filling the air, floating down to the carpet, absorbing into the fibres, staying there for years to come, like all the other conversations that have taken place in such storied walls.

Jesse is those walls, that carpet, the many posters decorating this foyer, soaking it all in, sitting and hanging and waiting, like he often does. Ever one to stay back, to wait and see. Often preferring to listen than to talk, enjoying the chance to be close to the star, but never be the star himself.

And he watches it all, patron after patron, engaging with Matthew, singing well-deserved praises, a revolving door of flattery, taking some time to thin out, but that time needed.

4

He's barely ready when his chance comes, trying as he might to find the right words, picturing his hoped end, but not knowing how to begin.

As the final hanger-on gives a wave, taking their leave, Jesse takes a big step, waving himself. Hoping his sudden movement will be noticed, never wanting to yell, to run, to be so bold as to assume.

The gesture doesn't seem enough, and with thick stickiness, he pushes out:

"Hey... May?"

Matthew snaps his attention, surprised and caught off guard, face dropping, expression plain.

Like hearing a once-beloved song.

Disbelief. And then. Flooding.

A tsunami of moments washing over Matthew. Dark eyes unblinking. Lips parting. Focused and unmoving.

"It's... Jesse..." He continues, taking another step, hands on thighs, leaning past the tipping point, second-guessing if this was a good idea.

Mathew's mouth forming the name, but no sound coming out.

"Is it... ok if I approach?" Jesse asks, hands coming up to cross his chest, prepared for every response but this one.

"...Jesse?" Matthew manages, blinking finally, breaking his own spell. "Yeah... yes."

Gap closing instantly, embrace tight as a vice, tears flowing before they can even be registered.

Like home, like comfort, like not even a second has passed.

But of course, it's been seventeen years.

# ARIA Top 100 Singles

# Year End Chart

# 2000

# No. 79

A temperate September. So Fresh CD blaring. Two small boys jumping and screaming on a big, soft, bed. Held together by tight hands.

The sanctuary of Jesse's house. An extra week off school. Matthew couldn't want for anything more.

He feels it. Something inside him settling. An absence of worry. A relaxing of his soul. Only around Jesse.

Red faces. Song coming to a close. Two small bodies tumbling into a bean bag.

Laughter. Like a hymn. Calling out to a higher power. Exorcising a buried hurt. Sitting deep in a young child.

Hand over hand, sweeter and softer than all the Melting Moments, in all the bakeries, shifting something inside and out.

Jesse smiling at him.

Matthew beaming right back.

The door swinging open. Tabitha strutting in. Turning the volume down. Glaring at Jesse.

"Get out of my room!" She commands, furious that Jesse had the absolute audacity to be in her room, listening to her So Fresh CD. "Get away from my stuff, you little doodle!"

"You're the doodle!" Jesse protests, getting up nonetheless.

"YOU'RE the DOODLE!" Tabitha shoots back, squaring up.

"I have a doodle!" Jesse throws, backing out the door.

"You're so GROSS!" Tabitha pushes back, walking him out the door. "Get out!"

Matthew frozen on her purple bean bag. Brain not communicating with body. Suddenly petrified.

"You too!" Tabitha turns, pointing to the door.

But he's unable. His legs won't. His arms couldn't.

Quick as lightening, Jesse runs back in, scooping Matthew up, rushing his small frame out into the corridor.

"W-why...?" Matthew blurts, unsteady on his small feet. "W-why was sh-she so...?"

"Well yeah, we shouldn't have been in her room, but like, whatever, aye?" Jesse shrugs, just a young boy who wanted to show off to his best friend. "But are you... ok?"

"...y-you said... i-it was ok." Matthew faintly states, defiant as he deflates, trying to claw at any reason, any chance to pull himself out of this hole. "You... lied?"

"I didn't... lie exactly..." Jesse stumbles, unable to look Matthew in the eye. "I'm allowed in there sometimes."

"I didn't like that... that Tab y-yelled at us..." Matthew manages, sinking into the cockatoo wallpaper, a whisper of a boy.

"Oh." Jesse folds, glancing at Matthew finally, seeing the whisper for himself, guilt driving into his tiny gut. "I didn't... I'm... May, I'm sorry. I didn't know..."

"I-I don't... w-wanna go in there... i-if... w-we're not allowed..." Matthew catches himself, barely keeping his balance. "Ok?"

"Yeah, ye-yeah, totally, ok." Jesse nods vigorously, reaching out, hoping to help, or at least not be a doodle.

Matthew taking the reach, pulling into a hug, eyes closing, like with Daniel, and yet completely different. A feeling so intangible, like trying to catch smoke with a sieve, so close to impossible, it might as well be.

"...two times one is two... two times two is four..."

"What's that?" Jesse asks, feeling Matthew's hushed words more than hearing them.

"...my times tables..." Matthew explains, returning to his reciting immediately.

"Well... after.... do you wanna watch more Olympics?"

Matthew only nods, up to his three's now.

# ARIA Top 100 Singles

# Year End Chart

# 1999

# No. 1

Matthew knows this is important. All the grown-ups say it's history in the making, as though it's something he'll be saying he witnessed, when he's a grown-up.

Oh, how he'll regale passersby, when he's old and boring, with the tale of this year, and it's rumours of aeroplanes falling out of the sky, because computers were going to stop working. And he was just a boy, but he was there.

But that's ages away, and in so many ways, he's just elated to be anywhere but home, and allowed to stay up past midnight. What incredible freedom, he's a big kid now, he'll even be double digits next year, and there's new stuff he gets to do all the time. Growing up sure does have it's perks.

A living room, six voices counting in chants, a unison of true festivity, Matthew looking to Jesse, preferring to watch his friend, than the countdown on the TV.

"...FIVE!"

Another number bouncing around the room, eyes watching the Harbour Bridge, here and around the country, waiting for the fireworks.

"...FOUR!"

Matthew seeing Vivienne and Leonardo holding hands, looking from each other to the TV, with such easy love, and in turn, reaching out to Jesse instinctively.

"...THREE!"

Jesse sensing something by his side, looking down to see Matthew's small hand, taking it with a smile, glancing up to those chubby cheeks. His other hand coming over to poke them, always so soft and warm, especially now, huddled inside with the Summer heat, and his entire family.

"...TWO!"

Chubby cheeks rising with a huge grin, Matthew squeezing fingers, wiggling his shoulders, natural and simple, just so happy to be here with Jesse.

"...ONE!"

The word so loud, pulling a single syllable into an entire sentence, filling the living room with such energy, sinking life into the beige chaise lounge, and zeal into the cockatoo wallpaper.

"...HAPPY NEW YEAR!"

Eruption. Cheering and clapping. So human to watch a clock and celebrate. To look forward to our small ceremonies. Chasing joy and connection wherever we go, whomever we are.

Jesse pulling Matthew into a hug, tight and ferocious. Just kids following an instinct to hold close, the one they feel closest to.

"Ew!" Tabitha shouts, pointing to her parents.

Matthew pulling back, assuming it was directed at he and Jesse, terrified of what might be coming next.

Vivienne and Leonardo pull apart, their small kiss ended. Vivienne's hand covering her lips, a smile behind fingers. Leonardo sticking his tongue out at his daughter, his whimsical response.

Matthew steadying, relief racing over him, an instant solace to his system.

"Yuck!" Tabitha retorts, giving her father a playful shove.

A raspberry in response, a smile to follow.

A laugh from Vivienne, barely heard over the blaring TV, filling the room with music and the scattering booms of fireworks.

Matthew taking it all in. A family playful in their teasing, loving in their raised voices, joyous in their retorts. So unknown, so fascinating.

Jesse reaching for his friend, arm around shoulder, wanting to be closer, not sure why Matthew pulled away, but probably just Tabitha yelling. But he's become so keenly aware his friend doesn't like shouting, even if it's not a big deal.

Matthew leaning into it, head on Jesse's shoulder, not a second thought about it, looking up to his comfort, in this small town, at the turn of the millennium.

"Happy New Year." He whispers, into only Jesse's ear, cutting through the commotion with surgical precision.

Jesse beaming down at his small friend, pressing his forehead to Matthew's, closing walnut eyes, at ease in darkness.

"Happy New Year, May." Jesse speaks, just for Matthew to hear. "You're my best friend."

"You're my best friend, too." Matthew replies, simple and true, as is so much at such small scale.

Excerpt from:

# WHEN

# THE PRINCE

# DOESN'T

# BECOME KING

Written & Directed

By

Matthew Seng

# SCENE THREE
# THE ARMCHAIR

**lounge room, armchair left of centre stage**

*WILLIAM is sitting in a large armchair, watching TV, smiling and comfortable*

## FADE IN – Orange Wash
## FADE IN – Audio Track 3 – 'TV Noise'

*JOHN enters stage left, drunk and unsteady on his feet, longneck in hand*

*WILLIAM immediately tenses up, smile gone*

*JOHN walks across stage, behind the armchair, then doubles back, approaches WILLIAM, standing over WILLIAM for a beat, back to the audience*

JOHN

[through gritted teeth]

Get out of my chair, poof!


*WILLIAM scurries out of the chair, off to stage right,*
*balling up in the corner*


*JOHN turns to slump into the chair, taking a swig*
*from the longneck*


[short beat]


JOHN

[casual yet forceful]

What are you fucking deaf

**and** a poofter?

Do you understand me?


WILLIAM

[shaky]

Yes. I understand.


*JOHN takes a swig*

JOHN

[spitting, spiteful]

Good.

It better not happen again.


WILLIAM

[shaky]

Ok.


*ZACH enters stage right, hurried and bold, he spots
WILLIAM cowering, and moves to help WILLIAM to
his feet*


ZACH

[calling from upstage, bubbling rage]

Dad! What the fuck?

[to WILLIAM, soft and caring]

Are you ok?


*WILLIAM nods, standing with ZACH's help*


*JOHN stands, tossing his empty longneck aside,
square with audience, turning head slightly toward
ZACH and WILLIAM, eyes narrowing*

JOHN

[righteous and aggressive]

Did you swear at me,

you little shit?


ZACH

[forceful yet controlled]

Yeah. And I'll do it again,

you fuckhead.


*ZACH gestures for WILLIAM to stay upstage. ZACH walks up towards JOHN, centre stage, holding position with rage*


JOHN

[through gritted teeth]

You little shit! I'll fucking-


*JOHN barrels up to ZACH, expecting immediate recoiling, anger in his entire body*


*ZACH doesn't back down, instead taking in a fiery breath. Chin up, shoulders square, looking through JOHN's eyes*

ZACH

[bold and rageful]

What?

You'll what old man?


*JOHN and ZACH square up, both with arms by sides*


*It's clear ZACH can match JOHN physically*


*JOHN assesses for a beat.*


*WILLIAM watching from upstage, looking back and forth, one hand on the back wall to hold himself up*


*ZACH holds his position, not an ounce of fear, ready to back up his words*


JOHN

[deflated but forceful]

Forget it.


*JOHN steps back, slumping into his armchair with a thud*

*ZACH remains towering over JOHN, eyes laser-focused on him*

JOHN (ctnd.)

[trying to hold onto his supposed "power"]

Get that poof out of here.

You've got 'til I

count to five...

ZACH

[aggressive, controlled, genuine]

You lay a hand on him,

and I'll kill you myself.

*JOHN waves dismissively, but just under the surface, he's shaken*

JOHN

[trying to have the last word]

five... four...

*ZACH turns to WILLIAM, putting an arm around WILLIAM. ZACH's body language is instantly completely softened*

ZACH

[reassuring]

Let's go, mate.


JOHN

[increasingly desperate]

three... two...


*ZACH and WILLIAM exit stage right*


**FADE TO DIM – Orange Wash**


*JOHN's eyes are busy for a beat*


JOHN

[desperate and angry]

...one!


**DIM TO FADE OUT – Orange Wash**

**FADE OUT – Audio Track 3 – 'TV Noise'**

# ARIA Top 100 Singles

# Year End Chart

# 1997

# No. 54

Eyes closed. Streams of salt. Refreshing like sea breeze.

Bronze fingertips pressing into sapphire linen, as Jesse feels the distance close, his forehead easing onto Matthew's shoulder, the light material greeting him there, so kind.

Matthew's hand moving to Jesse's neck without thought, comfortable, nothing to hold back, or keep to himself. Almond fingers sinking into dark brown shaggy curls, soft like clouds, thumb dancing back and forth. Needing that movement, even this tiniest of inches, something to remind him this is real.

A muffled, faint, thump. Some item fallen.

A step back. Like a stab to the heart. But this is no place for showing such a response.

Both looking down, fingers steady along arms, anything to hang on, to keep this going. They've both waited so many years, it can't be over so soon.

A bundle of denim staring up at the pair. A moment of processing. Another of realising.

"No way that's the same jacket?" Matthew asks, lingering gentle grip on Jesse's forearms, eyes fixed on the denim. "Is it?"

He glances back to Jesse, hoping against hope, his words don't cause him to sound so completely deluded, as to assume, this man would hold onto an item of clothing, for so many years.

And yet, so much of him wanting this man to be genuinely that sentimental.

Waiting. For a paused moment. To be correct, or to be corrected.

"Oh! Yeah, it is, hey." Jesse replies, jolting to life under Matthew's gaze, piecing the question together. "I kept stealing it from my dad and just... stopped giving it back one day."

The warmth filling Jesse's being, as he basks in his jacket's worthiness of being remembered, and hoping, with such ferocious hunger, to be equally as memorable.

"Really?" Matthew asks, the words soft as clouds, not brave enough to ask what he really wants to. "You held onto it... like, all this time?"

This could be his indication, his solution, but he can only dance around it, willing Jesse to take his hand and dance with him.

"Yeah it, um… it's older than me." Jesse smiles, lost in Matthew's onyx eyes, like swimming through deep space, plunging into oblivion, not as an act of falling, but as an act of floating, light as air, through the darkest dark. "And I didn't have the heart to…"

"Yeah." Matthew murmurs, eyes flitting to salmon lips, barely daring to imagine their taste.

"Mmm." Jesse hums, stealing a glance to full, blush, lips, wishing to float over to meet them.

A breath. Held tightly. Fingers sinking into it. Hoping to grasp the immaterial.

A gulp. Heavy yet buoyant. Impossible to keep down.

A moment. Paused and muted. A photograph in real time. Nothing moving, nothing heard.

Just flits and glances, wondering if and when and how, wanting and desiring, bubbling under such stillness. Just two souls alone, in a place meant for so many, falling into the liminal space, of only questions and no answers.

It's Matthew, with imaginings pushing down, as he so often had, who speaks into silence, who moves into stillness.

"Well that's…" He begins, thousands of unsaid words circling his mouth, attempting to pry their way out. "That's… really beautiful… you know, to… um… hold onto things… like that."

Jesse hears. Genuinely, truly. But second-guesses, presses back against his own conclusions. Double-speak falling from his teeth before he can stop himself.

"Yeah, I love it, so I wanted to hold onto it." He blurts, soft yet rushed, eyes tumbling to the denim bundle. "It's more than just a jacket."

Matthew feels a sharp breath rush into his lungs. He guesses, he hopes, he interprets. And maybe, just maybe, he's right.

But what if he's dead, fucking, wrong?

He watches Jesse's face, for a blip, a few frames in the film of his life. Only now, just here, as Jesse's eyes are down, and he can see without being seen, desperate to take in enough, but maybe it'll never be enough indeed.

That face, with skin of bronze, and warmth radiating from his cheeks. Walnut eyes down, to reveal full lashes, fluttering under a blink. Lips subtle but commanding, their salmon tones calling to Matthew. Could they be siren, or a lover's whisper in the night?

Matthew felt the tiniest jolt lift a finger, as the thought of holding Jesse's face in his palms coursed through him.

"Hey, let me." He spoke, trying to play off his imperceptible movement as something else, reluctantly leaving Jesse's forearms, and reaching for the storied jacket. "There you go."

"What a gentleman." Jesse flirts, hoping it comes through, waiting with wanting lips and restless hands, trying to burn the bush they were both speaking around. "And I haven't even given you the goods."

A flutter. A forced laugh. A bottle held up to the light, the message inside clear.

"I mean, I-I... I..." Matthew tries, words evasive to the writer, as is often the case. "It... that... and..."

"It's all good." Jesse reassures, seeing truth in Matthew's stumblings. "Just... saying thanks."

"Yeah... y-yeah, no worries." Matthew replies, hearing meaning in Jesse's clarity.

"Cool."

"Yeah, cool."

Nodding. Curt and Stiff. Lingering a beat too long.

"Congratulations on the play, by the way." Jesse saves, feeling the lull encroaching, and wanting nothing more than more words with the man he knew as a boy. "It was... really intense, but like, in the best way."

It's Matthew's turn to glance low, eyes finding the imperial red carpet.

"Thank you, that..." He begins, willing the words out, but they're sticky and hot, siracha on his tongue. "Means a lot from you. Though, I wish..."

He trails off, trying to piece it all together, hoping to come across as intended.

"I wish I could've known you were in the audience, but maybe..." He continues, again, finding such a disconnect between his thoughts and his words. "That would've got me in my head, I dunno..."

Matthew looking up finally, meeting Jesse's waiting gaze. Patient. Present. Pure.

"No, I get that." Jesse agrees, eyes bright and welcoming. "I get awkward when people are watching me in general, so I couldn't even believe how hard it would be with people you know in the audience."

A breath shared. An age bridged. A love coming back.

# ARIA Top 100 Digital Albums

## Weekly Chart

## 3 October 2022

## No. 29 (Track 4)

The guilt was a hell of a drug. Days and weeks and months and years, and Jesse gradually walking through it. Feet growing heavier and heavier, like boots becoming caked with layer upon layer of thick mud, dragging the body down, taking more and more effort to make each new step. Until the fact he was no longer worrying started to feel like it's own wound.

Where is Matthew? Does May ever think about him? Would the two even be able to hold a conversation now?

But most importantly: why?

Why did Matthew stop sending letters?

Jesse has his suspicions, his guesses, his own possible explanations. But no way to confirm. And with so many years past, would Matthew even want to see him now?

He should've done more, he wished against everything that he could've got May out of there, protected him from that house and that man.

And occasionally, like a shot to the heart, he'd watch a film, or read a book, or hear a song, that reminded him, not just of May, but of his inaction, of his childhood inability to fix things. Then and now.

There was a time where May was his whole world. Where those wide streets, with no traffic lights, and that tiny town, temperate even in the Summer, was the biggest thing he could conceive of.

And look at him now, stamps in his passport, stories wracking up, lovers and heartbreaks. A man of the world, holding a little part of himself free for a boy he knew a lifetime ago.

At first it was okay, the occasional phone call, and weekly letters, as though May was still around, despite the Nunes' moving to Sydney. And he was so little, still in primary school, just barely, he wasn't going to get on a train alone, not that there even was one to take to Oberon.

But it was a different time, there wasn't a computer in every pocket, kids didn't have phones, let alone numbers for them. Once a friend moved, there was only landline calls taken in the dining room, and handwritten letters, if parents would send them.

That was Jesse's first assumption. Peter Fletcher. He could even see that man ripping an envelope up in front of Matthew, and would hope against hope that he was wrong.

But all the same, the line was cut. And that was it.

He started high school, got busy with homework and new friends and Sydney things. Things he could've never done in a tiny town in the central west slopes and planes, where it snows in the Winter, and is barely warm enough for the communal pool in Summer.

No, he was a big kid now, and there was less and less space for May, like a hydraulic press squeezing gummy worms until they push out between the holes like silly string. Still present, but misshapen.

And he just wanted to be good at school, popular and great at English like Tabitha, or creative and a whizz at science like Alex. But he couldn't help it, he was just good enough at everything, solid seventy-something on every test, assignment, or exam.

Vivienne and Leonardo were always proud, celebrating his every win, as with his siblings', but he was floating for those years. And in every way, he knew it was likely because he never knew what happened to May.

It didn't help that the family moved again before Jesse started Year Eight. That was truly the nail in the coffin.

He hadn't heard from May for almost a year, but he still hoped.

And as everyone packed up boxes once more, and Vivienne reassured Jesse that she'd set up a redirect, and that he could still try calling each month, his heart just sank lower and lower with each rip of packing tape.

In his darkest moments, late into the night, when he was up working on an essay, he would ask his worst question: Is May dead?

Did Peter's rage cross a line of no return? Did May push metal into his veins? Is there a car with May crushed inside?

He always tried to push it down, not think about it, assure himself that he couldn't go there right now.

And by morning, or the next day, or the weekend, there was something else to keep him busy enough that he wouldn't ask those type of questions.

Three different times he let it bubble up long enough to write another letter, to try again, to reach out along the Great Western Highway, for a friend from another life.

Time, fickle and hilarious time, darker than ink and faster than bullets, looking back it seemed to crawl, and at the time it seemed to grab him under it's arm and run with him through his teens.

It's as though one day he woke up, had got his degree, and was writing emails and making calls, running for coffee, and resolving various stuff-ups, all while touring the world, never having to set foot on stage, but getting to be right along side bands he'd listened to as a kid.

Listened to with May.

He was busy again. Flying through his twenties like a heavy smoker through a packet of cigs, hungrily and quickly, reaching for another only to realise the packet is empty.

And the quiet. That intense silence of being at home for the first real time. His small flat was more of a storage facility, and a soft place to land, not really built for staring at walls until the night crept in again.

But needs must after all. Everything was shut down. And he just had to wait. Until curiosity got the best of him.

Laptop open, typing 'Matthew Fletcher' into every social media site he could think of, always coming up with some random white dude, that was absolutely not May.

Sure, some of them were hot, and Jesse absolutely would suck them dry, but that wasn't really an option right now.

He kept trying, in between streaming movies and emails about tours that were never going to happen, but he couldn't find his May.

Until one fateful October day, when something finally pushed itself out of a deep recess of his memory: Seng.

He paused the romantic comedy he was barely paying attention to, and opened a new tab, typing as fast as his fingers would allow: Matthew Seng.

There he was. Or a digital approximation, at least. Grinning and holding something. Looking almost nothing like Jesse remembered, but so noticeably the same person.

An undoubtable beauty.

The chubby cheeks have thinned, to reveal high cheek bones, but only from certain angles, for he still retained a youthful boyishness in his wide, rich, smiles.

Taller, brighter, with longer hair. Dressed mostly in tones of sapphire, iris blue, and zaffre, or occasionally, rich, vibrant, jade. Simple lines, artsy yet professional.

Always with a beaming joy Jesse has been deeply missing, and that he'd always tried to cause.

Zooming in, Jesse sees the object in May's profile is some type of award, and into the empty apartment he speaks:

"Fuck yeah, May!"

More clicking and scrolling reveals the boy he once knew is a playwright, and award-winning at that. All Jesse can do is continue to peruse, with the biggest smile his face has seen in eighteen months.

That is until he finds that a new play is opening next week.

A joyous scream escapes his lungs, standing and stomping with elation, soaking up the joy finding a friend after seventeen years. His body relieved, after crying out for movement, for newness, for joy, and before he realises, he's dancing.

Twisting and rolling, riding the wave of relief and happiness.

Less alone in this empty apartment.

# Yes, I Have

# Considered The Tetrapod

Hurrying behind a closing door, trying to catch his breath, and ease his brother down, carrying Matthew becoming both easier and harder as they both grow.

Those tiny feet unsteady on the floor, Daniel catching Matthew with a hand under the arm, dropping to carpet-burnt knees to assess the damage, on the outside at least.

"Hey... look at me, mate." Daniel soothes, checking Matthew's face for any broken skin. "Okay... it... it looks okay, but we'll check with Mum when she gets home, okay?"

'Mhmm." Matthew nods, chubby cheeks flat, face empty, an entire plane away.

Daniel bringing caring hands to tiny shoulders, rubbing thumbs over the soft fabric of Matthew's jade t-shirt, the one he used to wear, when his father used to seem untouchable. Not now.

"Are ya in there, May-may?" Daniel asks, trying to catch Matthew's thousand yard stare.

Huge, onyx eyes, fixed on the beige carpet in Daniel's room, unable to focus, distant. The information is before those eyes, but it can't be seen, not truly.

"May-may?" Daniel whispers, rubbing Matthew's upper arms, trying to will the mind back into the small boy. "two ones are what?"

Daniel pulling Matthew into his arms, holding close, his entire body surrounding the small, limp, frame. Trying, hoping, to be of some comfort.

It had worked before, so he's got a shot, but he's just a boy himself.

"May-may... please mate." He begs, trying to hold onto almost nothing, barely a being, more so a memory in his arms. "two ones are what...?"

A poster, coming into focus, figures in a black room, one standing forward, a pale face with hair, lipstick, outfit all in rich red hues. The image becoming clearer and clearer, and finally... Matthew can see it. He knows it well.

"Two... Day-day..." Matthew mumbles, onyx eyes on the Garbage poster, knowing where he is, and he's just a little safer here. "Two ones are two... two twos are four..."

"Yep, yep, they are!" Daniel praises, rubbing Matthew's back, relieved and settling, just a touch, but it's enough. "Two three's are what?"

"Two threes are... six" Matthew breathes, air rushing his lungs as he feels his body reanimate, his being returning to the realm of reality. "And... and..."

"And two fours are what, mate?" Daniel leads, smiling as relief washes over him.

"T-two fours are eight..." Matthew replies, bringing his arms up to hug Daniel back, finally. "And... two fives are... two fives are ten."

"They are! They sure are, May-may." Daniel confirms, eyes closing as he feels his embraced reciprocated, a brief respite from the fear of this house. "And two sixes are, what?"

"twelve... twelve, Day-day..." Matthew stumbles, leaning into Daniel's chest, soaking in the safety found here. "And two sevens are fourteen..."

"Yep, yep they are!" Daniel affirms, tears welling in the corners of his hazel eyes. "You're so good at this... and two eights?"

A hand pausing the compassionate back rubs, to wipe away a stream as it travels down his cheek, not wanting Matthew to see, hear, or feel him crying. The boy gets enough thrown at him, without needing to consider Daniel's emotions as well.

"Two eights are sixteen." Matthew answers, squeezing as hard as he can.

Daniel gasping, the effect small, the suddenness causing some surprise, but the best kind.

"They are." He praises, bringing a hand up to pat a smaller head, forgetting how much shorter the hair was today. "And two nines?"

"Two nines are eighteen." Matthew replies, burying his face further into his brother's chest, not wanting to be reminded of his new haircut. "And two tens are twenty."

"That's right." He responds, looking up to the off-white ceiling, willing the tears to stay in his eyes. "And two elevens are what?"

"twenty-two..." Matthew's muffled voice speaks, vibrating through Daniel's chest. "And two twelves are twenty-four."

A chin resting on top shorter, jet black, hair, breathing with his brother.

"They are... they are..."

Another escape. Another set of times tables.

Safe for now.

Excerpt from:

# WHEN

# THE PRINCE

# DOESN'T

# BECOME KING

Written & Directed
By
Matthew Seng

# SCENE SEVEN
# THE PHONECALL

**lounge room, armchair left of centre stage, corded landline on a small table far stage right**

*WILLIAM and ZACH are both sitting on THE ARMCHAIR*

*ZACH in the centre WILLIAM on the left arm*

**FADE UP – Orange Wash**

**FADE UP – Audio Track 3 – 'TV Noise'**

*WILLIAM and ZACH are leaning against each other, comfortable and at ease*

WILLIAM

[joking, pointing at the TV]

That's your girlfriend!

ZACH

[joking, light]

Oh yeah? Well, that's your...


*ZACH looks around quickly, weary, but bubbling with comedic joy*


ZACH

[whispering]

...boyfriend!


WILLIAM

[laughing]

Ewww! He's like... a thousand!


ZACH

[joking, only loud enough for WILLIAM]

Yeah, you like that!


WILLIAM

[laughing]

Ewww! No, I don't!

That's festy!

*ZACH and WILLIAM laugh, poking and pushing
each other playfully*

## FADE UP – Audio Track 6 – 'Phone, Landline'

*EVELYN enters stage left, slinging a tea towel over
her shoulder, she walks across stage to the ringing
landline*

EVELYN

[calm, clear]

Anak-anak, quiet now.

Telefon time.

*ZACH and WILLIAM fall silent, detaching from one
another in the playful fight*

*It's calm. Not a silence of fear, but a silence of love
and respect*

## FADE OUT – Audio Track 3 – 'TV Noise'

*EVELYN picks up the phone*

## PAUSE – Audio Track 6 – 'Phone, Landline'

EVELYN

[bright, clear]

Ya, hello?

## PLAY – Audio Track 7 – 'Neil Call, Landline'

AUDIO TRACK 7

[stumbling, strained]

Hello, um…is- uh…

is this… Mrs. Fletcher?

EVELYN

[suddenly tense, trying to hide it]

Ya… I am she.

AUDIO TRACK 7

[stumbling, strained]

Uh, yes… hello, Mrs. Fletcher,

I'm… Neil Baker, your- uh…

your husband's…

uh, I own the mill, and…

*EVELYN's face falls, her body freezes, she stares forward blankly*

AUDIO TRACK 7 (ctnd.)

[stumbling, strained]

He... today, uh... he was...

I'm- I'm v-very sorry...

*EVELYN looks, with eyes only, to ZACH and WILLIAM*

*ZACH and WILLIAM sense something, looking to EVELYN*

AUDIO TRACK 7 (ctnd.)

[clearing throat, strained]

Today, he was... he w-was

Fatally i-injured... on the job...

**VERY SLOW FADE – Orange Wash to Blue Wash**

*EVELYN backs up slowly, step by step, head shaking*

*Her knees give way, she drops to the floor. It's a
quiet drop, but heard through Audio Track 7*

AUDIO TRACK 7 (ctnd.)

[stumbling, strained]

We're... we're all very sorry

He... he is- he...

*ZACH and WILLIAM look at each other, sharing a
look of guilt. Asking, without words: 'did we kill our
dad?'*

AUDIO TRACK 7 (ctnd.)

[clearing throat]

Obviously... we'll take care of...

[stumbling, strained]

You and the boys...

we're a small... business, but...

I'll personally do...

Do everything I can to... to, uh...

*EVELYN drops the phone receiver, staring at the
floor, shuddering breaths animating her body*

AUDIO TRACK 7 (ctnd.)

[stumbling, dutiful, strained]

I'll pay out his, uh… salary for…

This year at least, then…

*ZACH jumps from his place, rushing to EVELYN's side, kneeling beside her softly, taking her hand*

AUDIO TRACK 7 (ctnd.)

[clearing throat]

Then, I'll talk to my accounts and…

[voice cracking]

We'll sort something out, okay?

*EVELYN continues to stare at the floor, heaving and crying*

AUDIO TRACK 7 (ctnd.)

[stumbling, voice cracking]

We'll take care…

of you and the boys…

w-we will.

*WILLIAM stares from THE ARMCHAIR, frozen and helpless*

AUDIO TRACK 7 (ctnd.)

[stumbling, strained]

Again, we're very... um...

*ZACH picks up the phone receiver*

ZACH

[raspy]

Hello?

AUDIO TRACK 7 (ctnd.)

[surprised, cracking]

Hello?

ZACH

[raspy, cracking]

What's wrong? Who is this?

AUDIO TRACK 7

[stumbling, strained]

I'm Neil, um, it's your dad, mate…

He… he was…

*ZACH goes blank behind the eyes, his assumption confirmed*

*A hurricane of emotions rushing through him, holding him still*

**Orange Wash to Blue Wash SLOW FADE COMPLETE – TOTAL Blue Wash**

AUDIO TRACK 7 (ctnd.)

[stumbling, dutiful, strained]

He… was fatally injured today

and we… we're gonna…

take care of you boys and your mum.

*WILLIAM continues to watch from THE ARMCHAIR, he knows. Somewhere inside he knows*

*EVELYN, ZACH, and WILLIAM are all still*

*The tableau is held until the AUDIO TRACK 7*
*DIALOGUE is complete*

AUDIO TRACK 7 (ctnd.)

[stumbling, strained]

We're... we're so very sorry

but we're... all gonna pitch in

and I personally am going to...

to make sure... you three are...

that you three are gonna be okay.

**FADE OUT – Audio Track 7 – 'Neil Call, Landline'**

**FADE OUT – Blue Wash**

## ARIA Top 50 Singles

## Weekly Chart

## 1 September 1991

## No. 19

"So rude, I haven't asked about you." Matthew proclaims, giving a squeeze to the shoulder, bringing his hand down and away quickly, feeling that the moment to linger has passed. "How are... what are... I dunno, you, right? And?"

"Couldn't have put it better myself." Jesse jokes, leaning in a little, adding a touch of flirtation. "I've been... good. I'm, um... a music tour manager guy... so, that's that."

"But that's cool, right?" Matthew asks, furrowing his brow playfully, feeling the familiarity coming back, gradually, but flowing. "Are you being modest? I won't allow such behaviour."

A small laugh escaping Jesse's lips, the display of attraction coming through. May giving him some shit, a little razz. So country, distant, yet familiar.

"Okay, alright. I'm kind of a cool dude. You got me." Jesse volleys, holding his hands up, jacket going with him, almost hitting Matthew in the face. "Oh shit, are you- fuck!"

A soft chuckle, light and joyous, tumbling from Matthew to the floor.

"You good?" Jesse checks, dropping the jacket to the imperial red carpet once more. "I don't need that anyway."

"No, I'm all good." Matthew confirms, bending to retrieve Jesse's jacket once again. "You can't go on without this, I won't allow it."

"I'm bi." Jesse blurts, eyes widening instantly as he realises the words that have just escaped his mouth. "I mean- I didn't- I'm... bi..."

"Congratulations." Matthew replies dryly, humour sitting just under his tone. "I'm gay, so... let's go queer community."

"Yeah, cool... I just... oh, thank you." Jesse stumbles, taking his jacket from Matthew. "And I... can I buy you a drink...? Somewhere... not here?"

"Of course." Matthew smiles, looking around to ensure no one else is waiting. "I just... have a few boxes to tick, but... if you don't mind waiting-"

"No! I can wait!" Jesse interrupts, before catching himself, and trying his best to adjust his volume. "I mean... that's completely ok. I can wait here."

"You're doing great, by the way." Matthew playfully affirms, leaning in a little, wiggling his shoulders for a little extra flair.

"Thank you, I'm trying literally so hard." Jesse replies, genuine and self-deprecating, his sweet spot.

"Well, look I'm gonna be as quick as poss, but it'll be like… fifteen mins." Matthew explains, bringing a hand back up, this time to Jesse's upper arm, giving a little rub, feeling that jolt of electricity, not wanting to let go. "Are you sure you're ok to wait?"

Jesse, knowing he has waited seventeen years, and can wait a quarter of an hour more, just smiles, glad his faffs haven't dampened his cool-guy-with-black-nails-and-tatts allure. It's truly all he's got.

"Of course, I have… I can… it's no worries at all, like, genuinely." He stammers, shooting for nonchalant, and landing nowhere near, a well-trodden path.

"Ok, I appreciate it." Matthew replies, basking in Jesse's awkwardness, enjoying that it lends something youthful, true, and new to this re-meeting. "I'll… be as quick as I can."

Matthew hesitating to go in for a hug, bringing his hand up to Jesse's shoulder, Jesse closing the gap, tight and fierce.

And then. Apart. Matthew disappearing. Jesse leaning.

The time crawling along, Jesse switching between apps, trying to will the minutes to pass quicker.

And thankfully, ten minutes later, a beautiful voice calls to him.

"Ok, you ready?" Matthew asks, appearing from behind a hidden door. "Where's good?"

"Oh... we could... I mean... if you..." Jesse stammers, wanting against everything to be alone with Matthew, like they used to, and completely unlike it as well. "M-my place?"

"Yeah. Is it far?" Matthew nods, his silent wish granted.

"Not really. Rosebery." Jesse explains, holding up his phone, lit up with a rideshare application. "And I... we can..."

"Yeah, rideshare is cool." Matthew agrees, glancing at the screen, and seeing the drive should only take twelve minutes, then jumping to clarify further. "I don't drive in, too much traffic before the show, you know?"

"Yes! I hate traffic too!" Jesse blurts, feeling his body trying too hard, and wanting to settle, to be chill, but feeling incredibly unable to. "Well... should I go ahead and... order it then?"

Matthew giving a quick nod and smile, then watching feverish bronze fingers select and nervously fidget, while he's calm and enthralled. Was this how he looked when the pair was younger? Jumpy and enthusiastic?

"Hey…" He says simply, hand reaching for Jesse's shoulder, settling on the black t-shirt, feeling the hot skin underneath, eager to soothe. "I'm really glad to see you. And I'm… really glad to spend time with you right now."

"Yeah?" Jesse questions, looking up from the light, and into the glorious darkness of Matthew's eyes, feeling his nerves settle, stress unfurling and dissipating.

"I don't mean to give you a big head." Matthew jokes, small smirk lifting the corner of his lips, looking right back into wide, walnut eyes. "But I don't usually go home with people after a preview."

The smirk becoming a genuine, beaming, smile, Matthew pulling a lip into a soft bite, watching Jesse looking up, glancing at those blush lips, not slick at all, enthralled as Matthew lets the bottom one escape his teeth.

"Yeah?" Jesse breathes, lost under Matthew's gaze, taking in this new-familiar face, and relishing in being the smaller one now.

"Yeah." Matthew flirts, watching himself be seen, be admired, and taking an enticing step forward, hand moving down Jesse's arm, caressing, meaningful.

The moment interrupted by a flicker of the screen, drawing Matthew's attention.

"It's here already?" He asks, both delighted and annoyed, all the better to get to Jesse's, but all the shorter to enjoy this twinkle in time.

"Mmm?" Jesse hums, blinking to attention, looking down at his phone. "Oh, yeah... we better..."

It's Matthew, with hand sliding away from Jesse, and backpack slung over shoulder, who takes the lead, heading out the art deco doors, to the late evening, inner west, city street.

Jesse following Matthew, resisting the urge to reach out and grab his hand, a mix of unease, and at-home comfort, washing over him.

"For Jesse?" Matthew asks, approaching the only car pulled up outside The Enmore Theatre.

"You for ride?" The driver enquires, leaning over the centre console, and speaking through the open window.

"It's Mohammed." Jesse elaborates, a step behind Matthew.

"Oh, sorry... Mohammed?" Matthew asks again, a shot of embarrassment coming up, which he swiftly brushes off. "For Jesse?"

"Yes, I am." Mohammed responds, pressing a button that elicits a click from the doors.

"I'll go in and shuffle over." Matthew instructs, giving Jesse a quick wink.

Hot excitement rushing over him, yet Jesse feels fear barrel through him too. Which is silly. This is May, and there's no way that boy changed for the worse. Further confirmed by the play Jesse witnessed barely an hour ago, though now it seems like last week.

Following Matthew, he slides in, buckling up, and giving a quick affirmation to Mohammed.

"So, how's... your family?" Matthew asks, as though this was just anyone, unsure what else to talk about with a third person in such close proximity.

"They're... all really good." Jesse lights up, happy at the opportunity to just babble. "Mum is retired, which is like... needed, she was getting swallowed up by work for a few years there."

"Nice. What did she used to do again?" Matthew follows up, wracking his brain for memories from the 1990's. "Sorry, it's been... too long."

"Oh, she's... well, she *was* a financial consultant." Jesse elaborates, recalling watching his mother rush out the door, as he was only just waking up, all through his teens. "So like... telling businesses how to better manage their money."

"Wow, okay... that sounds... very involved." Matthew replies, able to pull a moving image of Vivienne from this mind.

She's in pleated khakis and a ruffled white blouse, kicking off her brown Mary Janes, at the door of Jesse's house, during sunset, all through the Summer holidays. It didn't seem strange as a kid, but that would've been after eight p.m., and most of that time would've been driving, no doubt.

"Yeah..." Jesse continues, another flash of his mother coming into focus, sitting at a laptop well past midnight, nodding as he announces he's going to bed. "It did get a little dicey after we moved and-"

Jesse stops himself, he feels a fresh pain flood him, intense and heavy, like the drenching rain of the deep night.

Matthew hearing him, truly listening. Not just to words, but to everything else that he was saying in, and around, them.

His hand on the seat, crawling along the leather, the rest of him unmoving, watching, ready for any answer.

Jesse spotting the hand, swarmed with warmth in an instant, moving his hand reflexively, then with purpose, craving Matthew's touch like never before.

To finally be so close, like he thought he never would again, stretching over a tiny gap in the dark, in a strange car, after a lonely day, and a crowded evening.

Matthew extending a pinkie out, giving Jesse an offer, seeing if it'll be taken.

Jesse reaching in kind, watching their hands with thick anticipation, laying his little finger flat, wanting to be surrounded.

Onyx eyes watching Jesse's face, desire just beneath the surface, lips slightly parting, eyes fixed, yearning.

Pinkie reaching, covering another, curling around gently. Light, meaningful, tiny.

Jesse sucking in a thick breath, squeezing Matthew's little finger hard, glances wandering up his hand, to his wrist, to his arm, then shoulder, and finally landing on his warm, dark, eyes, watching himself be seen, the intensity flowing over him.

This is happening. This is real. May wants him too. And whether it's a night or a lifetime, he'll take it.

"Where is good spot?" Mohammed asks, gesturing to the dark street.

Jesse gives a final squeeze, wanting desperately to hold on, but needing to pull away.

"Oh, here is good, thank you Mohammed." Jesse replies, giving a buddy-smile to The Driver.

"Yeah, thank you." Matthew pipes up, already unbuckled and opening his door. "I hope you have a good night, Mohammed."

Closing the door softly, he stands in the street for a beat, taking it in, then rounds the car to wait for Jesse.

'Five stars from me." Jesse asserts, unclicking his seatbelt, holding up his phone.

"You two are very sweet." Mohammed softly speaks, catching Jesse's eye in the rear-view mirror. "I am also like you."

"You are?" Jesse asks, a genuine smile lifting his lips.

"Yes. We exist everywhere." Mohammed nods, hushed but assertive.

"We do." Jesse replies, opening his own door, joining Matthew on the nature strip.

# ARIA Top 100 Singles

# Year End Chart

# 2009

# No. 11

Synth bass barrelling from the tinny speakers of Tabitha's HP laptop, Jesse in his well-worn spot on her old, purple bean bag, in the sanctuary of her bedroom, with it's telemagenta feature wall, three bulletin boards clad with overlapping paper trinkets, and bookshelf teeming with CDs and school art projects.

"Hey... do you know..." Jesse tentatively begins, as he watches Tabitha apply lip gloss, the finishing touch to her make-up. "Do you know... what bisexual is?"

"Yeah, duh!" She replies, pressing her lips together, pouting, and blowing herself a kiss, in the small mirror of her bronzer compact. "I'm on Myspace! Everyone's bisexual there!"

Jesse looking to his feet, pressing them together where they overlap at his ankles, an attempt at venting nervous energy, wondering if he should ask his next question.

"And I'm pretty sure I am anyway." Tabitha continues, nonchalant as she stands and checks herself out in her full-length mirror, talking to Jesse's reflection as she continues. "It's like... at this point, if you're not bisexual you're like... boring."

Jesse looking up to her, as he has many times before, and will do many times after. And she, always bold and outspoken, never taking any bullshit from anyone, secure in who she was, making it look easy.

He wondered every day how exactly she did it.

With her colour-blocked outfits and choppy hair, never caring that people thought it was ugly, she wanted to rock this look, and she did. Though often Jesse just felt eclipsed by her, it was in the best way, able to hide in the shadow, where it's calm and temperate.

A sibling on either side, never the centre of attention, a state that was comfortable, if at times a little lonely. But maybe he could connect with Tabitha about this.

He watches her taking selfies with her silver Canon PowerShot, then checking them, mouthing along to a few lyrics between shots, then striking another pose. She truly makes it all look effortless.

"And... what if I was?" Jesse asks, watching Tabitha from behind for any negative reaction, any tiny movement, that would indicate his worst assumption. "Like... bisexual?"

But Tabitha doesn't flinch. She doesn't make a face. She barely reacts.

Maybe she didn't hear him?

"Yeah, you should be." Tabitha replies, continuing her selfies-and-checking routine. "Like I said, no one is straight anymore."

"That's... not what you said." Jesse mumbles, second-guessing any protest, but his mouth moving before he can quietly take the win.

"Yeah, but it's what I *meant*." She shrugs, rolling her eyes at this little doodle's inability to just get it the way she does. "Like, who's gonna be boring and straight, when they can be cool and bi, like? No one, come on."

Jesse soaking in Tabitha's oddly supportive words. They may not be directly encouraging, and they most often weren't, but he knows her intentions are always genuine.

"And you're not like... mad at me?" He quietly asks, only heard because the Lady Gaga song is coming to a close.

"For what?" Tabitha shoots back, looking up from her camera's preview mode, and popping her hip. "Doing exactly what I do all the time for my entire life?"

"Um... I was thinking more like being bi, but um..." Jesse stumbles, speaking clearer as a new song begins, willing to get this answer if it's the last thing his teenage brain does. "Are you mad about that other stuff?"

"Not really." Tabitha sasses, growing impatient with her little brother, but knowing he can barely help being so clueless. "I'd copy me if I could. I'm the best, Jess, like... be serious."

"Okay." He resigns, trying to work out if he even got his answer.

"Urgh, none of these are turning out." Tabitha protests, looking to her mimi pink ceiling, exasperated, then realising little brothers are good for some things. "Take some pics of me."

"Sure." Jesse agrees, happy to do something more in his wheelhouse – playing second fiddle to Tabitha – before posing an equally pressing question. "Do you think Alex is gonna be mad?"

"Huh?" She asks, in between snapshot clicks.

"Like, we're both bi, and that drongo is like... a boring straight." He elaborates, twisting his body to get different angles, having been adequately educated in the art of photography during a previous bedroom hang sesh.

"Let's wait and see." Tabitha dismisses, astutely noticing something about the youngest sibling years ago.

"What's that supposed to mean?" Jesse questions, putting the camera down for a beat to try and derive meaning from Tabitha's cryptic words.

"Nothing." She responds, gesturing for him to pick the camera up again. "Just let that derro figure it out."

"Okay." Jesse nods, complying with the request.

A few more clicks whisper out, and Tabitha holds out her hand silently, waiting to have her camera returned, ready to inspect and give feedback.

"Hey." She pipes up, clicking through the two dozen images.

"What?" Jesse asks, ready for his regular scolding.

"You know you were like..." Tabitha begins, still clicking through the previews, never looking up as she lays down the truth. "In love with May, right?"

"W-what... What?" Jesse responds, baffled by how this relates to the previous subject, and generally thrown from the lack of sibling bullying.

"Yeah, why would I be surprised you're bi." Tabitha shrugs, turning the camera around, showing off an image she likes. "You two were, like, married."

"Oh." Jesse concedes, the memory flashing before his eyes.

"Yeah." Tabitha sighs, taking solace in once again being right. "It's tough being the smartest person in this house. Now take some from a lower angle."

# ARIA Top 100 Singles

# Weekly Chart

# 21 January 1996

# No. 55

Jesse hanging his unused jacket up, and kicking off his black Vans, revealing bright pink kitten socks, peaking out from black cuffed jeans, before emptying his pockets onto a small table.

Gesturing for Matthew to do the same, with both sharing incomplete sentences, stumbling half-words, and several 'um' and 'ah' sounds, until Jesse pulls ahead, over to the kitchen area of his studio.

Walking cautiously into the small apartment, Matthew takes in the sunset ceilings and walls, adorned with posters framed in midnight blue, deep lemon, and kelly green, with two small armchairs around a circular table, to the far left, and a bed, made up with crisp, chalk white sheets, to the right, and beyond the inviting bed, Jesse is busying himself in the kitchen, off in the right corner.

But Matthew is pulled toward a small display shelf to his immediate left, with it's many knickknacks.

"What can I get you? A beverage? A little snackie?" Jesse asks, hands on cupboard handles. "Sorry this is so small, I'm on the road so mu-"

He cuts himself off, noticing Matthew looking and not touching, and knowing the impulse well.

"You can pick things up, nothing is breakable." Jesse encourages, pausing his cupboard-checking and leaning against the sink, to watch, perchance to gaze.

Matthew looking back wordlessly, taking a beat, then being overtaken by a wide smile.

He turns back, picking up a keyring reading simply 'Singapore', overlaying a painting of a beach at sunset.

"Did you get this in Berlin?" Matthew jokes, holding up the keyring.

"Ja, in der near von Berlin." Jesse replies dryly, taking a few steps over, but keeping a few paces between.

"Portuguese, English, *and* German, okay, he's a scholar." Matthew nods, wanting to keep the joke going, even if only to feel more comfortable in a new space.

"Well, I need a little of everything." Jesse shrugs, hands pushing into jean pockets, accentuating his shoulders and forearms. "It's good optics to do a little greeting, gets me more free coffee, and I love saving money."

Matthew hungrily looking over Jesse, trying not to show it too much, yet very sure he was blushing such deep carmine, it was approaching wine-dark.

"And I, uh…" Jesse continues, feeling explicit eyes on him. "Like to immerse myself, really get in there. So…"

"You're full of surprises." He smiles, glancing to the keyring again, unsure if this was really about to happen, and not wanting to get too far ahead of himself.

"I don't like to brag." Jesse responds, moving forward to lean against the wall next to the display cabinet.

"So…" Matthew starts, placing the knickknack back, and noticing Jesse out of the corner of his eye. "How was my motherland?"

"Oh, yeah. I've been a few times." Jesse perks up, pacing around behind Matthew, all the better to get a full view, then pointing at a MRT keychain. "That one is from my second visit in like… 2015, with Grrrl Sister. You know them?"

"No, but I need to." Matthew replies, turning to look at Jesse, almost close enough to lean in for a kiss, but not quite. "They sound like a cool punk band."

"They are!" Jesse responds, excitedly pacing back around, and over to point at one of his Grrrl Sister posters. "There's enough of a punk scene in Singapore to do a few shows in clubs, so I've managed Grrrl Sister for their…" Jesse, lit up like the Harbour Bridge on New

Years, points to a different, smaller, poster. "2015 and 2017 tours to South East Asia."

Matthew indulges in Jesse's excitement and joy, looking over the posters, containing three brown faces, with middle fingers up, and tongues sticking out, wearing some of the coolest outfits Matthew has ever seen. And he's worked in the performing arts for a decade.

"And what did you think?" Matthew asks, looking back to Jesse, still keen to find out his Singapore assessment. "Rate my roots right now."

"I didn't think we were gonna get right down to it, but I can get the lube." Jesse replies, shit-eating grin across his face, and eyebrow rising.

"Shut up!" Matthew retorts, more reflexively than anything, before actually registering the offer. "But later, yes." He nods, hands raising to emphasise the obviousness in his words. "But first, my homeland? Hello?"

The tone not lost on Jesse, and his vision blurs for a split-second, imagining the two naked and connected, before shelving those desires to answer Matthew's question at hand.

"Honestly, I'm working the whole time, so it's just like, where can I get food, or coffees, or stuff about accommodation." Jesse explains, wanting to satisfy

Matthew's curiosity before anything else. "There's not a lot of time for, like, culturally enriching activities."

"Hmmm. So you hate my people." Matthew flatly jokes, the corner of his mouth lifting the tiniest bit, giving his humour away. "I understand."

"I mean, best airport in the world how many years running?" Jesse sarcastically retorts, making a show of looking around for an answer to his rhetorical question. "Like a bunch. I do appreciate Changi, don't get me wrong."

"Hmm." Matthew jokingly narrows his eyes, before raising brows in agreement. "I guess so."

"Why?" Jesse volleys, one arm crossed, the other holding his chin in his best impression of An Intellectual. "Where's the essay you wrote about how much you love Singapore?"

"I didn't have to write it." Matthew jokes, holding his face in his own hands, trying to look as cute as possible. "Because I'm too pretty."

"I'll say." Jesse agrees, arms slack as he takes a few steps to Matthew.

"So you're like... a cool guy?" Matthew deflects, stepping out of Jesse's path, backing up towards the kitchen area. "You support women in punk, *and* you travel all the time?"

"It keeps me busy and around music, so I'll take it." Jesse answers, eyes lingering on Matthew's hips for a moment. "But you know, I'd be up for taking you sometime as well."

"Oh?" His interest piquing, Matthew pausing in his slow tracks. "Is that right?"

"Yeah. I like to bend over." Jesse shoots back, quick as you like, relaxed and flirty.

"A bisexual vers." Matthew nods, flitting between Jesse's form and his own nails pressing into the kitchen counter. "Kids these days really can't make decisions."

"And I'm a kink switch, so indecision runs deep." Jesse quips, crossing his ankles as he leans back against the wall, watching Matthew alternate between fidgeting and checking him out. "You better believe it."

"Kink you say?" Matthew asks, his fiddling stopping immediately, and dom-space washing his mind with easy clarity, onyx eyes boring into Jesse with possessive power. "What exactly... are you into?"

Jesse notices it. He knows he's in luck. That same intensity kept him enthralled with a Ms Right Now type a few years ago. And how he's always craved it. Hands on his body, ropes pressing into his flesh, nails on his skin, almost anything, pretty much anywhere, as long as it's intense.

The biggest adrenaline rush, waiting for him in any bedroom, or hotel room, or club toilet, anywhere in the world. But to be here, now, with someone who is both old and new, he's never felt lighter or more alive.

"Everything from like…" He answers, eyes on Matthew, bringing one hand up, across his thigh to his hip, pressing fingers into his jeans. "A little roughness, wrestling, pinning down, tying up, to like…" His hand travelling further, words falling out of his mouth with seductive ease, as he pauses on his décolletage. "Breath play, knife stuff and like… blood stuff."

The pink, purple, and blue, dagger tattoo on Jesse's right forearm taking on new meaning, as Matthew watches him change. Seeing Jesse fall into a role with such quiet vigour, waiting, hoping, putting on a little preview in the mean time.  Delicious, moreish, tantalising.

"So is that like…" Matthew replies, splaying a hand out on the kitchen counter, walking closer, allowing the hand to glide. "You want to be threatened with the knife or is it more of like… you want to be cut?"

"Both. Either." Jesse affirms, bringing his hand up to his throat, resting his grip there, staring wantonly over to Matthew. "But also, like… it's honestly quicker to list what I don't like."

"And what's that?" Matthew follows up, drinking in Jesse, imagining his own hand in the same position.

"I'd rather, you know, check out what's under the hood before I go for a ride."

"Mmm, I like that." Jesse responds, hand dropping, pushing himself off the wall, taking a step to Matthew. "Watersports, hardsports, vomit play, those are no-go's. It's a little... visceral for me."

"But someone cutting your skin and you bleeding is completely fine?" Matthew questions, deeply intrigued by this new side of Jesse, wanting to know absolutely everything he can.

"Honestly, it's like... blood, cum, and tears are hot for me... animalistic kind of..." Jesse replies, watching Matthew's hand gliding along his kitchen benchtop, wishing to have those hands on his skin. "But there's something that doesn't work about like... digestive track stuff... but I mean, that's exactly why it works for someone else."

"Yeah, I get that." Matthew nods, passing the end of the benchtop, reaching a hand up to lean against the wall, showing Jesse he can do it too. "It's like... blood, cum, tears, very dramatic, very theatrical, I'm listening. And I am aware of your bisexual culture and their penchant for vampires."

"Thank you for respecting our traditions." Jesse retorts, looking from Matthew's hand, down that entire body, relishing the thought of having it on him.

"So you're like... a bit of a freak." Matthew flirts, taking in Jesse's eyes on him, feeling the dripping desire waft over the few steps between them. "I wouldn't have guessed. But I'm... very happy to hear it."

"Yeah, I mean, happy to be a good surprise." Jesse flirts back, hands behind his back, absentminded but extremely true. "And what about you? Hard limits?"

"I guess so. I'm not super into bottoming. Not like... I mean..." Matthew answers, catching himself, all too aware of the unnecessary stigma, hoping to brush it off with some humour. "I care about bottom rights, I support bottoms, some of my best friends are bottoms."

"And we, in the bottom community, thank you for your support." Jesse replies, leaning forward, hands still clasped behind, prone and willing.

"And you're welcome to have it." Matthew volleys, another step, almost close enough to touch. "But it's like, I don't like not being in control. Pretty sure we all know why."

"Mmm. Yep." Jesse nods, leaning as far as his hamstrings will allow, teetering, pushing, trying to show off.

"Yeah, so it's like, more of a... sometimes thing." Matthew elaborates, taking the final step, a breath from Jesse, wanting to clarify he's not sealing the back door shut.

"Right, I get ya." Jesse nods, looking up through flirtatious lashes.

"But I like the wrestling and pinning type stuff." Matthew continues, bringing a hand up to Jesse's upper arm, tracing up to the compass peaking out of that black t-shirt on the left shoulder, feeling the heat through the fabric. "I'm surprisingly kinda buff."

"Is that so?" Jesse flirts, hoping he can be part of a demonstration.

"Are you..." Matthew begins, squeezing slowly into Jesse's traps. "Trying to get me to prove it?"

"Are you offering to prove it?" Jesse replies, feeling the squeeze continue, a steady, intense, increase. Delicious.

How he enjoyed the thrill, the chase, the uncertainty, and then that moment, that sureness, when everything lines up and it comes to clear fruition that the interest is mutual, and tonight is very much the night.

Excerpt from:

# WHEN

# THE PRINCE

# DOESN'T

# BECOME KING

Written & Directed

By

Matthew Seng

# SCENE NINE
# CHAIR THERAPY

**lounge room, armchair left of centre stage**

*WILLIAM is standing next to a large armchair,
looking over it*

**FADE UP – Spotlight – tracking WILLIAM
throughout**

WILLIAM

[thoughtful, reserved]

I did want you dead.

*WILLIAM paces away from THE ARMCHAIR*

*WILLIAM pauses for a breath, then turns, and paces
back*

WILLIAM (ctnd.)

[matter-of-fact, emotionless]

And, I'm... not going to,

to deny that...

I'm not a coward like you.


*WILLIAM points to THE ARMCHAIR, accusing*


WILLIAM (ctnd.)

[becoming angry]

But now you **are** dead, and it's like...

[laughing angrily]

Everyone is such LIARS!


*WILLIAM looks up, talking to the ceiling, exasperated*


WILLIAM (ctnd.)

[bubbling with anger]

Old people are such fucking liars.

It's disgusting.

*WILLIAM changes posture, embodying a character that is self-important, stubborn, and embarrassingly un-self-aware*

WILLIAM (ctnd.)

[imitating, mocking]

"Oh, you'll regret that when he's dead"

"You only get one father,

you should cut him some slack."

"Your dad does love you,

he just doesn't know how to show it."

[scoffs]

*WILLIAM flops down on the chair, exasperated by his own impression, and the weight of those past encounters with this character type*

WILLIAM (ctnd.)

[exasperated]

What an absolute sack of shit.

They're all just fucking lying,

all day, everyday.

[defeated]

Right to my face.

*WILLIAM gets up, very slowly begins pacing*

WILLIAM (ctnd.)

[angry and exasperated]

Knowing that I'm young,

and likely to believe them all.

And the worst part? **<u>I did!</u>**

*WILLIAM turns sharply to THE ARMCHAIR*

WILLIAM (ctnd.)

[laughing angrily]

I felt bad for wanting you dead.

[spitting and spiteful]

I actually felt sorry for you.

*WILLIAM again paces away from THE ARMCHAIR*

WILLIAM (ctnd.)

Thinking it must be...

[mocking, spiteful]

so hard.

*WILLIAM charges THE ARMCHAIR*

WILLIAM (ctnd.)

[accusing, pointing]

You know why?

Because you told me!

You told me it was

so hard to be a dad.

[voice cracking, pointing at himself]

To be **my dad.**

So hard to love **me.**

[recomposed, pointing]

You told me that shit everyday.

*WILLIAM again paces away from THE ARMCHAIR*

WILLIAM (ctnd.)

[sarcastic, angry]

But I'm not supposed to be sad.

I'm not **allowed** to be angry,

not at you.

Because that's not a 'real man'.

*WILLIAM pauses, far stage right, turns sharply to THE ARMCHAIR, stays in place*

WILLIAM (ctnd.)

[bubbling with both anger and humour]

No, a real man brushes it off,

keeps it inside,

harbours it for two decades

and unloads it on **his** kids.

*WILLIAM paces slowly toward THE ARMCHAIR, his gate is controlled, rage-filled, unnerving in it's ballet-like precision, each step even and exact*

WILLIAM (ctnd.)

[spitting words, bubbling rage]

That's what **you** did.

And you're a **'real man'**, aren't you?

[arms up, angry-calm]

Not me... I'm just a fucking faggot.

Oh, but you?

[laughs sarcastically, arms down]

WILLIAM (ctnd.)

[sarcastic, angry-calm]

Oh, you're **so** exceptional.

You would come home

like a hurricane.

Barrelling through the house.

Demanding space, taking it with force.

*WILLIAM reaches THE ARMCHAIR, hand on the
top, leaning in for effect*

WILLIAM (ctnd.)

[sarcastic, mocking]

That's a **real** man.

[laughs sarcastically]

Throwing a hissy fit

until he gets his way.

*WILLIAM straightens up, delivering to audience*

WILLIAM (ctnd.)

[sarcastic, mocking, angry-calm]

Very mature, what a great example you set.

WILLIAM (ctnd.)

[circling, hands up, mocking]

Storming around,

getting emotional

at the slightest little thing.

[stomping, hands waving, mocking]

Stomping your foot,

and raising your voice.


*WILLIAM relaxes, taking in a heavy breath, hands in*
*pockets, walks casually around stage*


WILLIAM (ctnd.)

[musing, genuine calm]

That'll show me

for being a gay kid.

That'll really teach Zach

for squaring up to you.

That'll learn Mum for being... what?


*WILLIAM turns on heel, far from THE ARMCHAIR*
*hands still in pockets, shoulders hitching, looking up*

WILLIAM (ctnd.)

[matter-of-fact, defensive]

Because she is

an absolute delight,

everyone loves her,

all my friends wish

she was their Mum.


*WILLIAM resumes walking casually around stage,
hands still in pockets, thinking for a beat, then
jumping to life, shoulders hitching again, gaze on
THE ARMCHAIR*


WILLIAM (ctnd.)

[matter-of-fact, defensive]

And not in like a

'she's nice when we have guests' way.

Which, you couldn't even do,

by the way.

No, Mum is a fucking rockstar.


*WILLIAM's hands spring out of his pockets, pointing
to THE ARMCHAIR*

WILLIAM (ctnd.)

[accusing, bubbling anger]

But she wasn't

good enough for... **you.**

[scoffing, pacing, sarcastic]

'Cause nothing

and no one is good enough for you.

Interesting that.


*WILLIAM turns, facing THE ARMCHAIR, hands behind his back, leaning to and fro, overstated and mocking*


WILLIAM (ctnd.)

[sarcastically musing]

Now I... can't help but wonder,

maybe no one was good enough for you,

**because** you think

you're not good enough.

Is that about right, dad?


*WILLIAM pauses, throwing up hands in a gesture of asking, looking around, waiting for a beat, as though someone is about to barrel in right now*

WILLIAM (ctnd.)

[simple, matter-of-fact]

You never felt good enough,

so you made that

everyone else's problem,

or, more specifically,

the ones you were supposed to

love the most, or even, at all.


*WILLIAM begins pacing around, in an imitation of his father's voice and movements*


WILLIAM (ctnd.)

[as exaggerated JOHN]

Yeah, the wife I asked to marry me,

and the kids I chose to have,

those are the people

who deserve the worst of me.


*WILLIAM stops, JOHN impression drops*


*WILLIAM heaves a heavy sigh, deflated instantly*

WILLIAM (ctnd.)

[heavy, emotionless, standing still]

Sounds about right.

And you couldn't help it, right?

You had a shit childhood,

so better pass it on.

Better make sure

I don't feel good enough either.

And Zach, and Mum.

As long as you suffered,

it's ok to hurt others.


*WILLIAM shakes his head, eyes high, heaves a*
*sigh, eyes on THE ARMCHAIR, he walks towards it*
*casually, emotionless*


WILLIAM (ctnd.)

[matter-of-fact]

What a cop out.

What an absolute

coward you are.

That's your shit,

you have to own up to it,

work through it, rise above it.

*WILLIAM starts walking away from THE*
*ARMCHAIR, turning to continue*

WILLIAM (ctnd.)

[accusing, measured]

You don't use it as an excuse.

*WILLIAM points to his chest, emphasising*

WILLIAM (ctnd.)

[asserting, measured]

And if I ever, ever,

chose to be a parent,

I'm going to be **nothing** like you.

*WILLIAM points to THE ARMCHAIR, punctuating*

WILLIAM (ctnd.)

[asserting, measured]

you will have existed

**only** to show me

the exact person

I don't ever want to be.

*WILLIAM backs up from THE ARMCHAIR, holding his gaze, walking backwards, calm with anger*

WILLIAM (ctnd.)

[spitting, anger under the surface]

Not even for a day,

not even for a **second.**

So I hope you enjoy

that sparkling legacy.

Although I guess sparkling

is too gay for a 'real man' like you.

*WILLIAM pauses for a moment, smiling with rage.
WILLIAM puts his hand to his ear, mocking*

WILLIAM (ctnd.)

[sarcastic and angry]

So what do you have to say? Oh?

*WILLIAM takes a big step toward THE ARMCHAIR,
holding for a moment, taking another, holding hand
to ear again*

WILLIAM (ctnd.)

[sarcastic and angry]

No scathing remarks?

No slurs to spit?

WILLIAM (ctnd.)

[another step]

No swinging fists?

Yeah, I thought so.


*WILLIAM rolls his eyes, scoffing, and walks far stage right, letting his father go as he walks, turning and leaning against the wall, looking over to THE ARMCHAIR*


WILLIAM (ctnd.)

[spiteful and victorious]

Because I outlived you,

you sack of shit.

I'll never forgive you.

I'll **always** hate you.


*WILLIAM stands tall, looking out, nodding and assured*

WILLIAM (ctnd.)

[strong, with slight smile]

And I get to control the story now.

So how about that?

*WILLIAM takes in a shaking, rageful, breath*

## TOTAL BLACKOUT – Spotlight

# 27 by American Rock Band
# Fall Out Boy

Eyes fixed on the screen, hand around his cock, pumping feverishly, trying to remain concentrated.

Jesse's mind wandering, his heart not in it, as much as his body cried out for release, and his soul ached for distraction.

He stops his stroking, the moans drilling right into his brain, their direct line, earphones – usually his most sacred self-love tool – proving to be a fresh hell.

Fingers grasping wires, and pulling quickly, not wanting to hear sounds of pleasure while his mind denies his own.

Eyes glancing down to his half-hard dick, thinking maybe something more forceful would do the trick, perhaps more sensation was what he needed.

The idea quickly pushed away, as he realises just how much work it is to torture his genitals, or wack himself with a flogger, or even just keep it vanilla, and ride a dildo.

He's over it. He's **been** over it for weeks.

Everything is an effort, a fruitless, never-ending, soul-sucking struggle. It's just him in this tiny apartment, wasting away with no end in sight.

And sure, he could call an ex-lover, text a friend, or even watch a stranger on cam, but that's all doing nothing for him in theory, so why would it do anything for him in practice?

He's just a pathetic little blob, who's wanked so much, he can't even cum anymore, all while he's barely able to bring himself to cook a meal, and hasn't had a real shower in days.

The alabaster ceiling, a reminder that he never got around to painting this place, bringing forth memories and moments. Flickerings of when he was vibrant, when he was a ray of sunshine, when he wouldn't think of not showering properly, even while on the road in a van with four band members, and barely enough in the budget for a can of soft drink from the servo.

Sure, he's been particular, even neurotic at times, but he always showed up, in every way, for his family, for his schooling, for his job, but now he can't even make his cock hard, or put garlic bread in the oven, or place a phone call to someone so dear.

And it's whatever, his body doesn't have to do one thing for him to enjoy it, there's so much more to pleasure and sexuality. And neither even have to be part of a full life.

But to Jesse, right now?

He just wants to do something, finish something, feel some sense of accomplishment. Even if that accomplishment is shooting a single rope from the tip of his dick.

But he spends most days in bed, watching movies until he gets bored enough to watch porn, and if he's lucky, he'll eat some cereal, or put some peanut butter on toast.

He can feel his life getting away from him, his light fading, his joy evaporating, and he's too lost to even find the handle, let alone be able to turn it, or walk through the door.

And maybe he'll try again in an hour, he thinks. Maybe he'll get up, and bake that garlic bread, that's been defrosting on the kitchen bench since breakfast. Maybe he'll finally call Clove back, feel that spark, the deep, pulsing, need, overtaking him, from hearing her sultry voice through the sky.

His soul screams for who he used to be, he'd crush his old self up, and snort it if he could.

But maybe he won't. No garlic bread. No call to Clove. No hanging onto his old self, like a widow keeping a photograph by the bed.

And in the indecision, in the grey, in the limbo between moving and stillness, he'll remain, for another day.

Kent Music Report

National Top 100 Singles

Year End Chart

1986

No.3


'Why don't you get on all fours…" Matthew suggests, pressing strong grip into Jesse's trapezius. "And we'll see."

The words hit like delicious venom. Potent. Powerful. Provocative

Jesse wordlessly complying. No more guidance needed. Falling to his knees with a fluidity and comfort of someone who's spent a lot of time sinking down. Walnut eyes fixed on Matthew, tiny smirk lifting up his lips, and fiendish tongue, unseen by Matthew, curling up to the roof of his mouth, then out to lick his lips, before biting it just a little.

With a thud, palms to the champagne carpet, muscles engaging, hoping Matthew can see them, they're not the biggest, but Jesse works out where he can, so he's proud to have a little definition. It's certainly helped in multiple similar situations.

Flicking curls aside to look up to Matthew, arching his back for good measure, hoping he's an inviting sight.

Matthew looking down at Jesse, good enough to eat, and he'd love to. With intention, he paces around, step by meaningful step, wanting to savour and taste the moment, from lip to lung.

Steps tight, tiny, Jesse can feel them more than see, trying to follow with his gaze, and failing after the first few, wanting to remain as still as possible, anticipation dripping off him. Lids closing, as he waits to feel Matthew behind him.

Turning on his toe, lifting heels, lowering down, controlled and purposeful, with palms out, Matthew's ready to make contact.

The smallest flash of skin showing between the blacks of Jesse's shirt and jeans, exposing an enticing piece of spine, Matthew's touch gracing it lightly, no pressure, just caressing, gliding, exploring, with legs doing all the work, holding, balancing, maintaining.

Fingers on his skin, sending tingles up his vertebra, sharp breath rushing his lungs, Jesse pushing back instinctively, wanting more, always more.

Knees on carpet, Matthew feeling the response from Jesse, pressing in ever so, guiding, commanding, teasing.

Pushing under fabric, just a little, short nails beneath the shirt, pausing for a moment.

"Yeah?" Matthew checks, low and sultry.

"Mmm, yeah..." Jesse coos, arching and aching.

Pressing further, crawling up, easing, feeling, craving.

Jesse sinking into the caresses, to have Matthew's hands on him, after all this time, of endless questions, of restless nights, of countless strokes to fruition, and now, he just wants to go anywhere with Matthew, ready for everything or nothing.

Other hand on shoulder, strong fingers pressing into sensitive muscle, pinching, intended to elicit pain, Matthew guessing with fingers, exploring with touch, savouring the sensation of seeing such a luscious side of Jesse.

All the while, busy gaze watching for any response.

"Uh-huuuh..." Jesse sighs, elbow buckling slightly, relishing in the sting, hoping to encourage a deeper grasp.

Both hands releasing, open palms, one on the small of his back, the other on his shoulder, Jesse waiting, eyes still shut, torso still arched, skin alight with desire.

Pushing down. Hard and sudden. Face to carpet. Body over body. Pinning. Trapping. Hips flush.

"...yeah..." Jesse whispers, eyes fluttering, cock twitching.

Matthew all around him. Larger, not by much, but enough. Enough to be at mercy, to be secured, to be completely enclosed.

Breath on his neck, that beautiful jet black hair gracing one cheek, while the other is pushed into the fibres of his carpet. Arms failing him, one tucked under, the other outstretched. Prone and helpless.

Chest against him, cock pressing against his arse, with only a few layers of material between, so close but so far.

He's on fire. Radiating heat. And huffing into Matthew's hair, as it hangs over and down to his face.

Matthew taking in a breath, a moment to marinade in this. The before, the anticipation, just to catch up to everything, and truly soak this in.

Jesse wiggling, trying to size Matthew up, hoping to get a good indication of what might be inside him soon enough. A cheeky little bitch at work.

Two hands slipping under two shoulders. Swift and unexpected. Clasping behind the neck in one fell swoop. Natural and easy.

Jesse locked in suddenly. Hands scrambling instinctively. Breath heavy.

"Yeah?" Matthew queries, ready to go further or pull back.

"Ye-yeah…" Jesse moans, sound coming out ragged, but delightful.

It's all Matthew needs. Pelvis pushing. Body to body. Heart beating between Jesse's shoulders.

Jesse breathing into carpet, completely engulfed, absolute heaven.

"Uhhh… huh…" He mumbles, speaking in the sensation of being at near-complete mercy.

"…you…aren't… you aren't… fighting…" Matthew breathes, hot on Jesse's neck, hair billowing as he speaks.

"I… don't… wanna." Jesse stumbles, palms floppy on carpet, lifting a foot, trying to playfully smack. "I just want… you."

Fingers releasing, tips tracing skin on the way out, Jesse sighing softly at the sensation.

Arms slipping through, touches running along skin, taking their time, Jesse feeling the pressure move to his hips, as Matthew rocks back and up.

Breath shaking Jesse under his touch, eyes delightfully closed, lips slightly opening, Matthew drinking the sight in, what a beautiful response, what a glorious human.

Weight on the knees, knuckles pressing into the carpet, lifting slowly, then all at once, a whine escaping salmon lips, no longer feeling the heaviness of another body on his.

"Flip over." Matthew instructs, simple and deep.

Jesse's eyes flashing open. Awake and alive.

Clumsy but fast, turning in the tiny space between Matthew's fists around his skull, and knees surrounding his thighs.

Onyx meeting walnut, Jesse swimming in the inky black, engulfing him, like he's falling right into Matthew. Lips waiting, palms facing up, chest rising and falling heavily, thighs pressing together, burning for pressure, for release.

Matthew ravenously looking over Jesse. Eyes on his, curls framing face, soft and yearning, shirt tight on a heaving chest, tiny glimpse of skin exposed between shirt and jeans, obviously hard cock just under the zipper, exquisite.

"You're so beautiful." Matthew praises, eyes returning to Jesse's, simple and profound. "So beautiful."

"You." Jesse says simply, more than a single word, an affirmation, a challenge, a compliment, a reply.

Smile turning up one side of Matthew's full lips, tongue pressing against teeth, ready to taste.

Pelvis lowering down, making gentle contact, then allowing weight to completely rest, close and needing.

Jesse tearing his stare from Matthew's eyes to those lips, feeling the arousal, the heat, powerful yet slow, they've had their whole lives, and now they're both here, what is there to do but take their time. Life is longer than expected.

Fists unfurling to steady palms, running along carpet, reaching Jesse's elbow, then upper arm, the skin soft, flesh burning underneath, fingers grasping around, sinking in, commanding and fierce.

Arousal to arousal, breath pushing against breath, expanding torsos with nowhere to go, chin gracing chin, just a little rough.

Matthew brushing top lip to bottom lip, feeling, more than hearing, Jesse's moan, as it moves from one to another, barely any space between.

Fingers squeezing flesh, mouths meeting at long last, true and starving.

A thousand stories told at once, tongues speaking without sound, wanting so deeply to be heard, to be felt, to be understood.

And finally, another to listen, to absorb, to reply in kind, like loneliness has never, and could never, exist.

Making up for lost memories, delicate and rough at the same time, exploring and forceful, reaching, grabbing, holding.

Matthew inching hands up to shoulders, under a burning neck, into soft curls, grasping firmly.

Jesse whimpering at such touch, needing and hoping for more, just a little more, and he'll be alright.

Pushing hips up, displaying and sensing, untouched hands flat and unmoving, waiting for instruction, to be shown, to be told, always wanting to be lead into bliss.

Matthew feeling Jesse's hardness, tightening his grip on those curls, breathing fervent desire into a hungry mouth.

"...cheeky bitch." He teases, barely pulling back enough for the words to come out clearly.

"I'll be anything you want." Jesse breathes, pushing pelvis up again, begging with both mouth and sex. "Anything, May…"

Matthew pulling back, just enough to watch a serene, glistening face, eyes closed, curls sticking to fiery skin, cheeks flushed, reddened lips mumbling 'anything' over and over again.

Hips grinding, watching air shudder into Jesse's beautiful face, waiting and burning for more.

"...yes…" He whimpers, behind the darkness of closed eyes, wanting to feel as much as possible.

"Yeah?" Matthew asks, hot breath pushing words over the biggest yet tiniest space between the two.

The reply coming in eager lips trying to meet, wanting to taste more, feel more, have more.

Matthew needing no further instruction, taking Jesse into a passionate kiss, tasting and feeling, torrid and hungry, pushing and grabbing and leading.

Travelling fingers along the carpet, trying to find vulnerable hands, meeting a forearm, dancing along the soft, fiery, skin, and into a waiting palm, fingers intertwining instinctively, grasping, holding, squeezing, tighter and tighter until it hurts.

Not to prove or overpower or flirt, but to connect, to let it soak. Matthew seeking to drink in as much as possible.

Jesse kissing back with voracity, head spinning, barely believing this is real, and wanting more than anything to just feel. A strong hand in his, fierce and surrounding, lips and tongue and breath on his.

Realising how alight is face is, as air occasionally brushes along burning cheeks, chest heaving, compressed by Matthew's.

Feeling the heat from deep inside, desire pressing against each other, feeling his and Matthew's at once, more than doubling it, legs prone and ready, under Matthew's spell and body.

Nowhere else he'd want to be, and nowhere else to be.

Matthew pulling back for a moment, looking over Jesse again, smiling.

"You are... I mean..." He muses.

"Took long enough." Jesse teases, trying to catch Matthew's mouth again.

"We've kissed before." Matthew breathes, lifting up playfully. "Don't you remember?"

ARIA Top 100 Singles

Year End Chart

2001

No. 21

Legs pounding, soft grass licking at exposed ankles, fresh October sun beating down, new to the sky, after hiding for the Winter.

Matthew reaching and grabbing Jesse, tackling him to the ground, landing hard on soft earth.

Jesse's body animated by hearty laughter, reaching up to tickle Matthew as his defence, despite being big enough to overpower.

Matthew giggling, squirming and wriggling, as several playful sounds of 'no' barrel out of him, tumbling to the side, rolling over onto the damp grass, looking up at the sky.

Jesse watching, reaching a hand out, palm to the distant cyan, rolling clouds reflecting back to him.

Another hand searching, finding. Matthew's fingers settling in between his friend's, fitting easily, smiling up at the glorious sky.

Quiet falling over the pair, the only two kids in the whole world, or so it seems.

Until the portable radio crackles with the voice of a B-Rock DJ announcing the next song, making some joke about not being too cool to enjoy a fun tune.

Bright and poppy, bouncing over to the pair, the lyrics falling from Matthew's lips.

"You know every song!" Jesse teases, looking to Matthew, always astounded by his friend's way with words.

"Just like, the good ones." Matthew brushes off, barely missing a syllable, eyes on the clouds. "Then I can sing along."

"You're so cool. You know so much stuff." Jesse praises, giving a soft squeeze to Matthew's hand. "It's cool."

"No, you!" Matthew throws back, squeezing in return, in between lyrics. "You're cool!"

"We can both be cool." Jesse replies, always keen to be as close as possible. "Together. The Cool Boys."

"That's us." Matthew agrees, tearing his gaze from the beautiful clouds, to look to a far more precious sight.

"Hey..." Jesse begins, walnut stare boring into deep onyx, trying to summon enough courage to finish his thought. "Do you think kisses actually taste like strawberry?"

"Huh?" He asks, focus split between lyrics and conversation.

"Like, in the song?" Jesse clarifies, giving another squeeze.

"Oh... I dunno. I've never kissed anyone." Matthew answers, unaware of any underlying meaning, taking the question at face value. "I mean, like I kiss my mum on the cheek, but."

'Yeah, me either." Jesse smiles, wishing to investigate right now, but hesitant to come right out and ask. "I don't know what kisses taste like... Just wondered."

Something clicking into place, becoming clear to Matthew. The words often needing a little more time, but when they fall in the right spot, they never move.

'I mean..." He tries, walking backwards into something uncharted, with hands over eyes. "We could... try?"

'Kissing?" Jesse beams, hoping he's hearing this correctly. "Like, each other?"

"Uh... yeah!" Matthew agrees, searching for a way to justify a simple curiosity. "Like, there's no one else around to kiss."

"Yeah, and it, like..." Jesse rushes in, grabbing at any and all straws. "Is just an experiment."

"We're like... doing science." Matthew affirms, preparing his own explanation, should it be needed.

"Yeah, science." He nods, sitting up, their hands never separating.

Shuffling for a moment, Matthew sits up too, moving to face Jesse truly, the two in sync, mirrors of each other, legs crossed, knees and shoes touching. So close in the vast backyard.

"Yeah… so… how do we do it?" Matthew asks, not wanting to make a fool of himself, this 'experiment' feeling suddenly so important.

Jesse moves closer still, and rush surges through Matthew as knees rub up against each other, causing his toes to curl inside his FILA runners, one of Daniel's many hand-me-downs.

Having Jesse this close, like this, has him feeling all giddy. It's different. And exciting.

"In movies they like… press their lips together." Jesse explains, holding his hand up, making a fist, and facing his thumb to his face. "Like, if this is you… then I'd go like…" He continues, bringing pursed lips to the space between his thumb and index knuckle, holding for a beat, then pulling back. "And that would be a kiss."

Matthew watching, feeling that rush again, trying not to show it too much, unsure if it's something he should be experiencing, or not.

"Right…" He nods, trying to play it cool, and barely making it. "I just… I think I'd want to be the one to…

like..." He explains, leaning in almost enough to touch his lips to Jesse's, then tilting back.

Watching wide-eyed, with tummy flipping, Jesse feels funny, good-funny, as Matthew moves close then back, wanting more than anything for that to happen again, for real this time.

"Yeah, that's good." Jesse confirms, feeling his voice go higher than usual, but more concerned that his flipping tummy might be visible to Matthew.

"Okay." He nods, licking blush lips, glancing to Jesse's, hoping he can do a good job. "Well... ready?"

Jesse feeling light, as though he might float away if Matthew doesn't kiss him right now.

"Yep. Do it." He agrees, voice steadier this time, but good-funny sensation very much present and accounted for.

Matthew squeezing again, both palms sweaty all of a sudden. Looking over Jesse, that rush barrelling through him once more, stronger, and he likes it. With lips pursed, and right hand on Jesse's shoulder, he's ready to be a scientist.

"Okay..." He braces, eyes closing, breath unsteady. "Coming in now..."

Moving closer slowly, scared, worried, but mostly excited. Just needing to know, wanting to find out, it's all just a test, it's just like mixing chemicals or something. It's not a big deal.

Pursed lips meeting, a tiny pause, nowhere near long enough, and he feels silly, charged-up, and airy, all at once.

Jesse awash with good-funny, his calves pressing together, his hand squeezing Matthew's fingers tight.

And pulling back, two boys looking awestruck at each other. A beat. Quiet. Knowing more and less simultaneously.

"That..." Matthew starts, knowing exactly what to say, but not wanting to speak too much truth. "Didn't taste like strawberry."

"...yeah." Jesse agrees, feeling fluttery, floating just a brush above the grass. "But it was... kind of... nice?"

Matthew beaming. It **was** nice. And Jesse thought so too.

"Do you wanna..." He begins, feeling just courageous enough to speak a little truth. "Try it again?"

Jesse nods. Short and enthusiastic. He'd sell his soul to do it again.

"Okay, close your eyes." Matthew instructs, giving a rub to Jesse's shoulder. "Here I come."

Leaning in again, pursed lips meeting anew, eyebrows raising, hearts racing together, beating in sync, faster and lighter.

Jesse squeezing hand in sweaty hand once more, trying to hold on.

Matthew squeezing back, pressing fingers into Jesse's shoulder, hoping to keep steady.

Jesse reaching, in the dark, in the middle of the day, and landing on Matthew's knee, soft and special.

It's so short, but so sweet.

Lips separating, eyes opening, nervous giggles escaping, awkward gazes looking off in different directions.

Matthew pressing his lips together, feeling them tingle, an unknown sensation in his stomach, mind running rampant.

But a look to Jesse, and he can feel himself settle. His home, his heart, his first kiss.

# Kent Music Report

# National Top 100 Singles

# Year End Chart

# 1982

# No. 3

"We... did?" Jesse asks, wracking his brain, trying to recall the memory, cursing himself for packing it away somewhere unreachable. "But... when?"

"It was... I don't know, like... a year before you left, maybe less." Matthew answers, rubbing his nose against Jesse's. "You don't remember?"

Jesse deflating, an all-too-familiar guilt washing over, threatening to drown him.

"Hey... hey..." Matthew asks, releasing his grip from Jesse's arms, and propping himself up onto elbows. "Where are you going?"

"Mmm?" Jesse replies, trying to find Matthew, reaching through the thick waters of his own emotions. "Going?"

"Yeah, like... mentally, emotionally." Matthew clarifies, lifting his leg, trying to roll off Jesse as gracefully as possible.

Reaching a hand over, dancing light touches along Jesse's arm, between the 'Ordem e Progresso' just above his elbow, and the pumpkin peaking out from his t-shirt.

Jesse feeling it, but distant, as though Matthew's hand and his arm were both covered, a glove trying to rub a jacket, present, but evasive.

"Wh-what do you mean?" Jesse asks, one foot in the void.

"Like, are you here right now?" Matthew clarifies, craning his neck to watch Jesse. "Or are you in your head?"

"Mmm?" Jesse hums, wading through the thick waves, legs heavy in the water. "Yeah, I'm... I'm good."

"Are you sure?" Matthew asks, giving light, rhythmic taps to that arm, his tether to Jesse. "You don't have to rush."

Jesse feeling the worry clearing, just enough for him to see the route out, a path that avoids the rips, his chance to wade his way ashore, muscles tensing and pushing, feet kicking up sand as he heaves onto the beach, tumbling to the ground, and finding himself back on his floor, Matthew next to him.

"Yeah, I'm..." Jesse starts, not sure how to finish. "Hey."

"Hey to you." Matthew replies, giving a tiny squeeze with his thumb and index finger.

"And thanks." Jesse mumbles, mouth feeling unpleasantly new. "That was nice."

"To literally care about you drifting off?" He asks, propping up onto his side, looking over Jesse with concern.

"Yeah."

Thousand yard stare peppering Jesse's one word with a hundred stories.

"Who's not doing that?" Matthew follows, returning to his tiny touches.

"I don't know... people... exes, colleagues, whatever." Jesse shrugs off, staring blankly to his kitten socks. "It doesn't happen much, anyway."

"Do you ever..." Matthew begins, hoping this will come across caring and not condescending. "Talk about this stuff?"

"What stuff?" Jesse mumbles, wiggling his toes under the bright pink socks.

"Like, I just brought up a cute moment, and you don't remember it, so you..." Matthew wades, moving delicately, touches even more so. "You go off somewhere... maybe somewhere... not great?"

"Yeah, but that's... normal." Jesse replies, the words coming to him sparingly, knowing he doesn't have to find the best ones as quickly as he can. "Right?"

"What's 'normal'?" Matthew proposes, not wanting to feed into that particular well tonight. "But maybe it's not... the healthiest."

"...oh."

"Like... I have a therapist." Matthew elaborates, each step soft, and he's ready to retreat at any moment. "And so does Daniel, like in the play."

"The play..." Jesse absorbs, blinking into his apartment, looking to Matthew. "That was... real?"

"Yeah. Most of it." Matthew agrees, happy to have a familiar detour. "My dad's been dead for ages and his legacy is I'm trying every day to not become him. That's the play."

"Oh." Jesse repeats, eyes travelling back to the pink kittens.

"Yeah, it was the biggest relief of my life." Matthew elaborates, remembering the lightness he felt after that phone call from the mill. "And everything has been uphill from there. I mean, who did you think it was about?"

"I didn't..." Jesse considers, seeing the connection between the stage and memories that should've occurred to him sooner. "I guess I just enjoyed it and... like, I was thinking about it after, but like, I guess I didn't think to myself like 'I wonder if this is based on real events or not', you know?"

"You're in the minority there." Matthew informs, recalling invasive questions from strangers, continuing his feather-light touches along Jesse's arm. "Audiences love to speculate, I get the weirdest DMs."

"Oh." Jesse says once more, a sudden urge to keep those 'weird DMs' far away from Matthew, to protect this man from anyone's invasions at any time.

"But it's like..." Matthew muses, shaking random messages from his mind. "Good that you can just see it as art, and not try to like, I don't know, mine my life for details."

Jesse nodding, hearing, absorbing, allowing his brain to catch up to the connection between art and experience.

"And when you write about it... that helps too?" He asks, eyes moving to watch Matthew's hand.

"Yeah, it does... it's also like... if I broke my knee, I wouldn't just need help right as it breaks." Matthew explains, halting his tracing, resting fingers inside Jesse's elbow, thumb tracing over the raised skin of the 'Ordem e Progresso'. "But I'd also need to go to physio and stuff, so it's like... therapy is like that."

"...right." Jesse nods, mostly here, a little gone. "Your dad's dead?"

"Yeah." Matthew beams, always relieved to live in a world without that man. "Pretty great right?"

"I mean... he wasn't... nice."

"Yeah, one less abusive bigot." Matthew muses, watching Jesse's stare get longer.

"...yeah."

"And there's also a grief, a sadness..." Matthew continues, thinking back to his time on Yolanda's couch. "But like... therapy, so..."

"But I haven't had like..." Jesse begins, transfixed on socks once again. "Something like *that* happen."

"I mean... you forgot we had our first kiss in my backyard during the school holidays..." Matthew recounts, hoping his findings are being presented well. "Maybe there's a reason you forgot."

"What do you mean?"

"Maybe there's some complex emotions..." Matthew puts forth, hoping he's not getting too lost in the weeds, before Jesse can identify the forest from the trees. "And your brain erased that moment, to... to make it easier."

He knew that was right. He knew Matthew could see him, and wasn't going to bullshit him.

Maybe this is the time. Maybe this is the place. He won't know until he tries.

"I thought you died." Jesse confesses, detached and matter-of-fact. "I thought... I didn't hear from you, because you died."

"What?"

"No, that sounds bad- it's like... sometimes I would think... maybe..." Jesse tries, feeling hot again, but in the far more unpleasant sense. "I hadn't heard from you... and couldn't find you online... because... you were dead."

"Oh... like, my dad did it?" Matthew follows, picturing the fists coming at him, the image holding no sting anymore.

"And- I guess, like..." Jesse continues, the words flowing now. "Everything I ever watched about queer characters... they all die."

"Yeah... that's... yeah." Matthew agrees, a rapid-fire of images shooting to his minds eye, queer suffering as cinematic spectacle.

"So, I just... when you said... and I couldn't remember... I just kinda, like, I would think sometimes, I should have..." Jesse stumbles, the end on his tongue, but he's scared, even here, even now.

"...what?" Matthew asks, calm and curious, not a pinch of harshness. "Should've... what?"

"Saved you." Jesse admits, the guilt doubling in his mouth, wafting up to his brain, direct and painful.

"I mean... that's so incredibly loving, genuinely, really." Matthew replies, hoping to hit that sweet spot, the delicate balance of communicating clearly without straying into insult. "But... I mean... you knew I had mum... and Daniel, right? Like, I had two other people in my corner. I was gonna be okay."

"But I was a kid..." Jesse tries, feeling tiny and silly, baking under his own embarrassment. "And when I say it now... fuck it sounds morbid, and I would try so hard not to think about it, not to go there... but yeah... a few times."

"That's a lot." Matthew observes, watching those far-off eyes.

"It is?" Jesse asks, slowly turning, finding a caring face waiting for him.

"And you had nowhere to put that?" Matthew leads, hoping to offer what he can. "No journal, no therapist... did you speak to your family about this?"

"No." Jesse confesses, watching himself be watched, revealing and intimate.

"But they're all so nice." Matthew pushes gently, wiggling his fingers in the crook of Jesse's elbow, a playful encouragement to stay with him. "Like, even your dad."

"Yeah, it's just..." Jesse starts, gaze snapping to the touch, trying to catch up to when those fingers settled in. "I was still figuring out... you know..."

"Mmm. Bisexuality strikes again." Matthew jokes, jiggling vigorously, shaking Jesse's entire arm.

Small, genuine chuckles roll from Jesse's lips, awaking his ribs, his neck, his jaw, moving him back onto his carpet truly.

"Shut up." He volleys, giving Matthew a teasing push, not enough to disconnect the grip, never that rough.

"I can." Matthew smiles, a laugh just under his words. "Any time. You let me know."

Jesse nodding through his final chuckles, hand resting on Matthew's, anything to hang onto his tether.

"And hey, look at us." Matthew asserts, thumb stroking up to Jesse's palm. "You thought I would be like... some tortured broken artist, but maybe... that's you."

"Hardly." Jesse brushes off, never one to claim much of anything. "I'm not creative like you."

"Your job is problem solving." Matthew pushes back, not about to let Jesse diminish a single thing, not while he's here. "Nothing more creative than that."

"I do it for the t-shirts and posters." He jokes, pushing a laugh out, another attempt to distance himself from himself.

"I do it for the coke and threesomes." Matthew replies, not entirely sure how much humour that holds. "How about those drinks?"

"Wow, putting me to work." Jesse blinks, giving a final rub to Matthew's hand and easing himself up onto his elbows. "I was warned about you bossy twinks."

"You're more of a twink than me." Matthew throws back, guiding Jesse up, then giving a playful squeeze of the neck.

"I'm too little." Jesse protests, pouting his bottom lip and bringing shoulders up to his ears.

"Twinks are little, you absolute idiot!" Matthew volleys, easing his hand out from between shoulders, giving a playful shove. "How long have you been fucking men?"

"Why?" Jesse shoots back, sitting up properly, Matthew's hands showing him the way. "You need references?"

"Yeah, I wanna read the Yelp reviews." He dryly replies, touch tracing all over Jesse, somewhere between comfort and flirtatious.

"Yeah, the listing is 'Jesse's Tight, Hot, Arsehole'." He jokes, falling into the comfort of Matthew's wandering hands. "It's four and a half stars."

"Why'd you lose the half star?" Matthew jokes, pausing with one hand on sternum and the other between shoulder blades.

"Not enough of a twink." Jesse returns flatly, tiny curl on once side of his lips.

"Walked straight into that one." Matthew remarks dryly, before pressing in a little, and shaking both hands firmly.

Jesse's eyes fluttering closed for a beat, the jiggling on either side of his heart bringing an instant jolt of alertness, along with a sensation of deep calm.

"Walked gay into it." He laughs, bringing fingers up to surround Matthew's heart-hand.

"This is bad for me." Matthew jokes, circling his grip in place, absentminded and caring. "They're gonna come take away my writer's licence, or worse, my gay card."

"I did my paperwork, but never sent mine in." Jesse jokes, his voice shaking a little, but becoming more bright with each word. "That's the bisexual way. You wouldn't get it."

"True, true." Matthew agrees, sarcasm lacing his words, his circling coming to a stop, hands remaining in place. "Working in the arts for over a decade, I've never met a bisexual person, so it's hard for me to wrap my head around your wacky lifestyle."

"And I appreciate you trying so hard." Jesse returns, jovial tone falling as he continues. "It means so very much." He adds, soft smile curling salmon lips, his words carrying double meaning. "The entire community thanks you."

"And I'd love to thank them back." Matthew volleys, tilting in, resting forehead on temple. "But I'm a little busy having a drink with you right now."

Jesse laughing softly, Matthew all around him and yet giving him space, teasing, and yet showing such love.

He rises uneasily, wanting to be of use, get those much hyped drinks. And it's Matthew's hands, again, as they guide, help, soothe, simply by virtue of their presence.

Excerpt from:

# WHEN

# THE PRINCE

# DOESN'T

# BECOME KING

Written & Directed

By

Matthew Seng

# SCENE FIFTEEN
# THE MARRIAGE

**lounge room, empty**

*EVELYN and WILLIAM are walking around the empty room, contemplating the years spent in this home*

*Slow and quiet. Bittersweet*

**FADE UP – Orange Wash**

WILLIAM

[unsure, but trying]

Mum?

EVELYN

[light, neutral]

Mmm?

*WILLIAM pauses his walking, leaning against the wall, upstage left, behind where the ARMCHAIR would be. His eyes are fixed on the phantom ARMCHAIR*

WILLIAM

[trepidatious]

How were... things with you...

and dad?

*WILLIAM looks up from the spot, over to his mother*

*EVELYN pauses right centrestage, her head turns slightly to WILLIAM, her eyes are lower, but not on the floor*

EVELYN

[attempting to avoid pain for WILLIAM]

Sayang...

WILLIAM

[trying to push, only a little]

Please, mum... was he...

ever good to you?

EVELYN

[with pity, lovingly dismissive]

Oh, Sayang… he was…

a complicated man.


*WILLIAM rolls his eyes, visibly annoyed, not of EVELYN, but of everything that would cause her to respond with these words*


WILLIAM

[barely composed, almost scoffing]

That's putting it lightly.


*EVELYN considers for a moment, not WILLIAM's words, but her own. Eyes still low*


EVELYN

[nodding blankly]

Ya, it is. He had…


*EVELYN takes in a full, meaningful breath. It's heavy, and takes a few seconds to fill, then empty, her lungs*

EVELYN (ctnd.)

[flat]

...a deep terror in him.


*WILLIAM begins slowly pacing, small and controlled, eyes low but gaze meaningful, bubbling with rage and hatred for his father, and the actions that hurt EVELYN, HIMSELF, and ZACH*


WILLIAM

[resigned, with cold rage]

Yeah, I'm familiar with his terror.


EVELYN

[correcting, gentle]

No, for himself.

I could see. He was...

[with pity]

Scared of himself. And he...


*WILLIAM pauses in place, he is still far from EVELYN, and looks to her slowly, listening*

*EVELYN looks up and off with a lapping spite, strong
and constant like calm waves*

EVELYN (ctnd.)

[with lapping spite, resigned]

Took it out on us.

Easier.

*WILLIAM sinks, realising the extent of his mother's
quiet, deep, rage*

WILLIAM

[even, matter-of-fact]

But that wasn't right.

EVELYN

[nodding slightly, rage-calm]

It wasn't.

No, it wasn't.

*EVELYN's face becomes animated, but her posture
and body language remains restrained*

EVELYN (ctnd.)

[explaining calmly, commanding gravitas]

But, Sayang, you have to know...

For me, for women like me...

We are lucky to...

[empty eyes, resigned]

To have any man.

We are in **debt** to the man.


WILLIAM

[rushing]

But... but...


*EVELYN interrupts, but it is with the same
commanding gravitas, WILLIAM knows he was the
one who spoke out of turn*


EVELYN

[calm gravitas]

It's... different now.

And I see him for what he was.


*EVELYN's words sink into the stage, a brief pause, a
processing beat, quick but meaningful*

*WILLIAM hearing, truly taking in the words, savouring this rare candour, but rushing to defend EVELYN*

WILLIAM

[protesting, baffled]

But you... deserved better.

He was- he-

*EVELYN nods slowly, eyes closed, she hears WILLIAM's words as intended – love for his mother*

EVELYN

[with a weak smile]

I know... I know now.

*WILLIAM contemplates not speaking, but he knows he must. During a pause, he is subtly animated, eyes looking back and forth, mouth beginning to open twice*

WILLIAM

[matter-of-fact]

Well, I'm glad he's dead.

*EVELYN hears WILLIAM with almost no reaction*

EVELYN

[plainly]

Me too.

*WILLIAM looks to EVELYN, relieved yet saddened*

*EVELYN looks to her hands for a moment, smiling
weakly. She doesn't see WILLIAM*

EVELYN (ctnd.)

[plainly]

When I saw how much better his boss

and the other workers treated me...

not even my own man, stranger man

but they did so much,

bringing me pay cheque, mowing lawn

and their wives, saved me...

bringing me food,

having you boys stay,

talking to me, taking me in...

*EVELYN tears up slightly. She bites her lips, trying to keep herself from crying. It's the relief of no longer being afraid, of experiencing kindness, it's hard for her to keep from crying when she's safe and happy*

EVELYN (ctnd.)

[with voice cracking]

Like I was like them

everyone in this town was…

*WILLIAM hears the cracks, his face sunken, watching, frozen and unsure what to do. He just listens. **It's enough***

*EVELYN clears her throat, presses her lips together, trying to take a moment to attempt to compose – to be, and remain, steady*

EVELYN (ctnd.)

[clearer, with some cracks]

Better to us than…

he ever was.

but I didn't know.

I didn't know until I saw…

*EVELYN clears her throat again, trying to slyly wipe a stray tear, she looks up to the ceiling, taking in a shaking breath*

*WILLIAM continues to watch, incredibly still*

EVELYN (ctnd.)

[trying to push through tears]

Until I **had.**

That's when I knew...

what I didn't have.

*EVELYN's feet remain planted, but she turns her head, trying to again wipe a tear slyly. It's seen, just like the first one*

*WILLIAM takes one step, then stops, scrambling, trying to form words*

WILLIAM

[with such deep love and no pity]

Mum... I never knew...

*EVELYN sniffles, forcing a smile, moving finally. She walks to downcentre stage, waving dismissive hands*

EVELYN

[shaking head, sniffling]

Of course you never knew.

You were child, I care for you.


*EVELYN can't bring herself to look at WILLIAM, trying to gesture hands towards him. Her end position almost blocking him from the audience*


*WILLIAM stands upstage left centre, a step to the side of EVELYN, but from some views, truly behind. He hears her words, protective love washing over him, holding him in place*


EVELYN (ctnd.)

[firm and reassuring]

**I** worry about **you**.

Your job is school and play.


WILLIAM takes a few steps forward, reaching for EVELYN, he's two steps away as he speaks


WILLIAM

[protesting]

But, I-

EVELYN

[with protective love]

There is no 'but', Sayang.


*WILLIAM stops, a step from EVELYN, arms length*


*EVELYN feels his presence, and can tell her words
stopped him. She turns to WILLIAM (still cheating to
the audience, head turned more than body),
considers him for a moment, then continues*


EVELYN (ctnd.)

[with protective love]

It was **easier** without him.

And you were a child.


*WILLIAM can only watch, take in the love EVELYN
is offering, the love she has offered a million times
before in a million ways. He nods softly, smiling the
tiniest smile*


WILLIAM

[simple and clear]

…thank you, Mum.

EVELYN

[with soft love]

Oh, Sayang… come here.


*EVELYN closes the gap, taking WILLIAM into a hug
full of unconditional love, and a cutting, shared pain*


**FADE OUT – Orange Wash**

# ARIA Top 100 Singles

# Year End Chart

# 1998

# No. 23

"Do, you Matthew Fletcher, take Jesse Oliveira Nunes to be your wife?" Tabitha asks, hand on Matthew's shoulder, gesturing to Jesse with a copy of Uncanny by Paul Jennings.

"Why does he get to be the wife?" Matthew objects, stomping feet, with palms held gently in Jesse's.

Tabitha, swimming in her father's suit jacket, rolling her eyes, towering over the younger boys, annoyed by questions from her two players.

"Because! You get to wear the dress, you doodle!" Tabitha huffs, throwing the paperback up in frustration. "We already agreed!"

Matthew's knees wobbling, bouncing in anger, billowing the floral fabric of Tabitha's dress.

"But if I'm wearing the dress, I should also get to be the wife!" Matthew shoots back, hands never leaving Jesse's. "I want to be special!"

The words not sinking in, not quite coming through to such young souls. As those raised with love aren't often attune to the depths of small protests made by those raised on survival.

"But you get to take your briefcase and make money." Jesse brings up, more of an attempt to end the disruption than to soothe a protesting Matthew. "That's really cool!"

Jesse beaming down at Matthew, nodding along, hoping his response convinces those wobbling legs and chubby cheeks.

Matthew looking from Jesse, to an impatient Tabitha, to his hands, in Jesse's, warm and loving.

Maybe being a husband is a small price to pay. And he looks so pretty now, so perhaps he can take this in stride, like so many other slights.

"Ok fine!" He concedes, pouting a fat lip to Jesse, hoping for more kindness. "I'll be the husband!"

"You're gonna make so much money!" Jesse praises, sincere and naïve, but as true as he knows. "The best husband!"

"Okay..." Matthew mumbles, gaze falling to his socks, then to the dress.

Smiling at the large sunflowers against such vibrant blue. At least he gets to be all dressed up, the one everyone would fuss over and notice. It's so nice, even if it's not real.

Jesse doesn't even get to be all pretty, he's just wearing a denim jacket the three stole from Leonardo's wardrobe, over his baggy t-shirt and trackies.

"Good!" Tabitha huffs, wanting to get back to the ceremony for the waiting, packed, audience – her dolls. "So, do you, Matthew Fle-"

"I do." He interrupts, smiling up at Jesse.

"No!" Tabitha cuts through, as only a teenage girl can. "You don't say anything yet! You wait... and you listen!"

Matthew about to recoil, unable to decern between someone being temporarily upset and someone barrelling toward him down the corridor, ready to lay fists upon his flesh.

But it's Jesse, like a thread of loving salvation, connecting him to the mortal plane, that pulls him back.

Forehead leaning down, laying on held hands, gentle and simple. Without urgency, intuitive and loving, not to cut Matthew's response off, but to show an oft scared boy, that he's not alone in his own darkness.

"Okay, okay, you're a very happy couple, I get it." Tabitha relents, rolling eyes unseen by a bowing Jesse and a watching Matthew. "Let's go from the start."

An affirming murmur from Jesse, head raising up, smiling softly at a now-settled Matthew, both ready to start over. Anything to stay here a little longer.

# ARIA Top 100 Singles

# Weekly Chart

# 5 March 1995

# No. 72

"I remember I used to tell my dad all the time that you and I were gonna get married." Jesse mentions, reminiscing in the moonlight, nudging Matthew, shoulder to shoulder.

Matthew raising an eyebrow, but able to hide it, continuing to look out into the swaying leaves, waiting for the other shoe to drop, and hopefully it wouldn't involve a proposal.

"And I think, he thought... it was like me saying that I wanted to marry my favourite TV character." Jesse continues, a tiny laugh lifting his words, as he lays a head on Matthew's shoulder. "Like, I think he didn't think it was genuine... like, feelings."

"Yeah..." Matthew begins, trying to find the words that are actually true, not just the defence his brain often goes to first. "It's weird looking back and being like 'all the signs were there', but I guess... it wasn't so obvious at the time."

The sentiment floats out into the cooled air, and around to Jesse, those signs flashing up in a moment, projections onto the dark, every tiny way he has always been so far gone for May, without even realising.

Just a kid, wanting desperately to spend every second with another, and how he wasn't to know, not back then.

'True, it was the 90's…" He retorts, rubbing a smiling cheek into the soft fabric of Matthew's midnight blue hoodie. "So I guess queer people hadn't been invented yet."

'Yeah." Matthew agrees, happy to hopefully be steering away from something so serious. "We came into being in 1997 with the premiere of Will & Grace."

'Karen Walker made me bi." Jesse jokes, bringing a hand around to Matthew's opposite shoulder, wanting to sink in, to hold on, even in flippancy. "Let the right-wingers know!"

Matthew laughing, bringing palm to waist, and hand to cheek, lapping up the post-rain night air, in the concrete box that is this balcony, in the exquisite company that is Jesse.

"I'll get every right-winger on the phone right now." He volleys, giving a little pinch to Jesse's cheek.

"Yeah, you've got them all on speed dial, right?" Jesse returns, playfully pushing against Matthew's palm.

"Oh you know me so well." Matthew impishly replies.

He turns to Jesse, who follows easily, the mirror and the mime, attuned to each other as only such known souls can be. And he reaches, tenderly and with ease, running fingers through curls, smiling down at bright walnut eyes.

The hot spell may be broken, but the heat in that stare is still scorching. And it lingers, how it always lingers, unable to get his fill, having been deprived for so long.

Jesse buckling just a touch under it, trying to play it off with a quip.

"It's why I wanted to marry you." He tries, before rushing to clarify, only realising his words after they leave his lips. "Not now, though, just like... to make that clear."

Silently screaming onyx eyes relaxing, as Matthew sighs a heavy exhale, uncomfortable laugh not far behind it.

"Oh, thank-"

"Not that... oh, you're-"

"Not into marriage either?" Matthew interrupts, overlapping Jesse's overlaps, admiring the space left in the wake of a ripped-off band-aid.

"Oh good." Jesse sighs, suddenly tonnes lighter, but eyes finding his kelly green slip-on Bin Shoes regardless. "I've had exes that took it as like, hating them or something, which like… hey, people have their damage. But… it's not for me."

Unfavourable tableaux flicking past his mind's eye, a View-Master of faces during arguments, sometimes his fault, other times not as much, and the touch of death: Clove Venkadeshan.

But he blinks it all away, not wanting to move from this present truth to a skewed past.

"Yeah, same." Matthew replies, overjoyed to agree on one of the biggest items on the list, as he talks to Jesse's dark curls. "Not the exes part. It's not gotten that far."

"To talking about marriage?" Jesse enquires, snapping up, curiosity peaked.

"More like…" Matthew begins, recalling his many hook-ups and flings, a collection of connections. "Into being a relationship."

"Oh shit, right." Jesse concedes, unsure if this could be a sore spot.

"Yeah, something about being fairly emotionally-unavailable and an absolute workhorse hasn't granted me long-term relationship status." He jokes, smile curling the very corner of blush lips.

"Right." Jesse laughs, glad to have not hit anything.

"Which in Gay World is like... three months." Matthew adds, ever more comfortable in this tone, following this throughline.

"Oh, down from six?" Jesse jumps in, grinning.

"Yeah, it's a door buster sale." Matthew volleys, settling into the easier realm of banter.

"Those are my favourite." Jesse smiles, before that curiosity gets the better of him. "But like, marriage aversion... can I ask why?"

Waiting with breath held tight, wondering, as onyx eyes look up to yet more concrete. The tiny balcony surrounded by it, and Jesse watches that gaze follow it all around, and look out into the sharp contrast of the mid-February evening after a much needed downpour.

"Yeah, it's half like, general relationship anarchy, and half sort of..." Matthew muses, looking to Jesse at last, with thumb coming up to drift along a waiting jaw, index finger settling on chin, gazing at his boyfriend truly. "We as queer people shouldn't have to like... emulate straight culture to be seen as worthy of basic humanity."

"Yeah, I hear that." Jesse agrees, pursing salmon lips, eyes closing softly.

Blush lips closing the small gap, kissing gently, simply, with an ease the speaks more of the years spent apart, rather than the mere months together.

"And you?" He asks, running that thumb along Jesse's bottom lip.

"I mean... basically the same." Jesse replies, content smile lighting up his face under the single overhead light. "Straight culture is like... painting with two colours, so why would I want to be part of that?" He continues, looking out to the soaked leaves, thinking of the rain's power to elevate colours, just like him. "Like, even when I've dated women I've been like 'I'm a bi disaster, please respect that...' kind of thing."

"Gotta respect the bi disaster hustle." Matthew quips, watching a staring-off Jesse, enjoying the thoughts he gets to hear, and the ones he gets to see.

Jesse turning back to Matthew abruptly, a devilish look on his face, as he quips:

"It's hard out here for a bi-di!"

Glorious laughter erupting from Matthew, belting and thick, defiant in it's intensity.

Heavy bellows coming from Jesse, layering into an energetic exchange, throwing back and forth with glorious passion.

Untamed. Unrestrained. Unashamed.

# ARIA Top 50 Singles

## Weekly Chart

## 23 August, 2004

## No. 28

"Sayang, how you today?" Lydia asks, greeting Matthew after school, wanting to give him all the love inside her, today of all days. "School good?"

Matthew deflated. Exhausted from his first day without Jesse. Sure, Daniel kept an eye on him, but it just made him feel more like a helpless baby.

And he's a big kid now. He's *not* a baby. He doesn't need this constant minding.

"It was okay, Mum." He replies, kicking off his shoes, and slinging his backpack down to the tile. "How about you?"

"Oh, the practice always same. People come in, sit down, see doctor, pay – always same." Lydia dismisses herself, waving hands and giving a sly huff. "But you, Sayang, good day?"

Matthew absorbs it all for a beat, allows himself to see the dots joining into lines, and the intention behind his mother's greeting.

"Is this about... Jesse?" He asks, knowing the answer, perceptive beyond his years.

"Well ya, how about Jesse?" She asks, having noticed the pair's closeness. "You two... very special friends... so maybe..."

"Um..." Matthew scrambles, feeling his entire body burning, suddenly his school polo and dress shorts are too heavy, a thermal blanket in a wildfire. "W-wha...?"

"He was... special type of friend... so maybe you..." Lydia tries, wanting more than anything to put this into the right words, knowing it's not the language barrier this time. "And I-... I'm here, Sayang... I love you."

"I love you too, Mum." Matthew rushes, skin superheated, sweat beading everywhere uncomfortably. "And I have... homework, so..."

Grabbing for his backpack, he dodges past his mother, and dashes into his room, closing the door swiftly and quietly, not wanting to seem too distressed.

Heart pounding. Bag dropping. Body sliding.

On the floor he sits. Head swimming with a million questions. And only one answer: He can't like-like Jesse.

Not here. Not now. Not ever.

And how could his mum know? What did he say, or not say? Was it how he walks, or how he talks?

Should he have been more interested in sports? Maybe less? Too much of watching other men has got to be a little fruity, right?

Or did she know he was writing again? He tried so hard to hide it, how could she have noticed?

Should he have said more things about girls bodies? But he's only just started high school, surely that's not expected now, right?

Did his dad know?

He couldn't, right? The man is always too busy yelling, drinking, or out yelling and drinking somewhere else. It's a wonder he finds the time and sober hours to make his shifts at the pine mill.

There's no way that man knows.

And maybe Matthew's mum doesn't even know anyway. 'Special Friend' could mean anything... right?

Hoping for a distraction, Matthew reaches for his school bag, and rummages around for his maths homework.

A sheet of paper, wedged between the pages of his exercise book, with fractions and multiplications. This he can handle.

Simple. With a possibility of a clear answer. Much better than the questions in his head.

# ARIA Top 50 Singles

# Year End Chart

# 1988

# No. 35

"Meu Pequeninho! How was your first day?" Leonardo asks, handing a peeled carrot to Jesse. "Did you make any new friends?"

"Yeah, I guess..." Jesse shrugs, slicing the carrot, slow and focused, like he's been taught. "The kids were nice. Or... seemed nice."

Jesse's efforts go to waste, as Leonardo is too smart for this act, seeing right through his son.

"You know, Pitoco... it would be ok if you miss Matthew." Leonardo reaches, giving his son the option, and hoping the boy will take it. "He was a good boy, and I think... a good friend to you, sim?"

Jesse focusing on his father's hands peeling vegetables, rather than look the man in the face, hearing Leonardo's words, but unable to find his own.

"...yeah." Jesse tries, not so much taking the offer, as observing it's existence.

"Sim, so it's ok if you're a bit sad." Leonardo reassures, bringing Jesse's cutting board over to a pot, and tilting the contents in. "Or even... very sad."

"Sim, Papá." Jesse replies, watching the carrots, celery, and potatoes tumble into the broth.

"And I love you, and your mother loves you." He affirms, returning the board to it's spot in front of Jesse, with knife on top, blade facing away, as always. "No matter what kind of friends you have, or even... when you're old enough... what kind of person you love."

Jesse nodding, looking to his empty cutting board, realising he does feel excited about Matthew, just like the men he sees on TV. But that's probably normal, to want to be as close as possible to a friend.

Leonardo hoping his intention comes through, gesturing for Jesse to come stir, placing a comforting hand on his son's shoulder.

"Whatever you do, and whoever you are... te amo."

Jesse nodding, feeling something inside him settle, something that he can't quite reach, as though his arms aren't long enough yet, but maybe some day soon, he'll grow tall enough to pull it in, with the very tips of his fingers.

"I love you too, Papá."

Excerpt from:

# WHEN

# THE PRINCE

# DOESN'T

# BECOME KING

Written & Directed

By

Matthew Seng

# SCENE NINETEEN
# THE GRAVE

**empty stage, headstone centre stage**

*EVELYN, ZACH, and WILLIAM enter stage right, walking towards THE HEADSTONE*

*EVELYN is carrying a single white rose, wrapped in plastic*

**FADE UP – Green Wash**

*EVELYN pulls ahead, ZACH and WILLIAM hanging back*

*EVELYN places the rose down, and stares at THE HEADSTONE*

*A silence falls, it's awkward, hanging for around thirty seconds*

*EVELYN looking about herself, then back to her children*

EVELYN

[commanding, saddened]

Anak-anak come now.

*ZACH and WILLIAM hurry to either side of EVELYN, also looking down at THE HEADTSONE*

EVELYN (ctnd.)

William, you are so good with words,

you say something?

WILLIAM

[stumbling, uncomfortable]

Ah, yeah... of course...

Well... I guess, um...

despite everything,

I am sad you're gone.

And... the older I get,

the more I realise,

how much you missed

WILLIAM (ctnd.)

[stumbling, uncomfortable]

by being so closed

and so cold... um...

*EVELYN reaches for WILLIAM's hand, he takes hers, ZACH watching, and reaching out to take her other hand*

*EVELYN nods to WILLIAM, urging him to continue*

WILLIAM (ctnd.)

[stumbling, more uncomfortable]

Well... it might be...

hard to feel too sorry for you

but I do wish, um...

*WILLIAM turns to EVELYN*

WILLIAM (ctnd.)

[apologising]

I'm messing this up.

EVELYN

[encouraging, lovingly minimising]

No, no...

You're saying all perfect.

Please keep... Please go...


WILLIAM

[stumbling, searching]

Okay, um... this is... um...

this is the man... who...

[clears throat, he's got it now]

this is the man who holds us all together

and that's his greatest legacy

he would've never

achieved anything greater

in almost every way

but we... as the ones

able to live on are freed...

in- in his death

and for having known him

have learned so much

in the hardest manner possible.

[deep breath in]

WILLIAM (ctnd.)

[stumbling, searching]

But, um… we grow,

we heal, not because of

but in spite of you

and we have each other

not because of

but in spite of you, too.


*EVELYN leans a shoulder towards WILLIAM,*
*sniffling softly*


EVELYN

[with every ounce of love possible]

That's very beautiful

you did very good job.


*WILLIAM smiles at his mother's touch and praise, he*
*looks to her with endless love and thanks, but he's*
*all out of words*


WILLIAM

[smiling, depleted]

Thanks, mum.

WILLIAM (ctnd.)

[gesturing to ZACH]

Do you... wanna say anything?


*ZACH wipes away a tear, taking in a cleansing breath, shaking his head*


ZACH

[shaky, steadying as he speaks]

No, you... you said everything.

And better than I ever could

and there's nothing nicer

to say about...


*ZACH gestures with his free hand to THE HEADSTONE*


*EVELYN nodding in response, standing up straight, pulling her children in for a group hug*


**FADE OUT – Green Wash**

# ARIA Top 100 Singles

# Year End Chart

# 2007

# No. 60

A rusty hinge, squeaking out into the December air, sun beating down onto a hopeful new adult, searching for something he's been waiting on.

And a letter, addressed to one Matthew Fletcher-Seng, with an important piece of paper inside.

He grabs it, leaving the hinge to drop the letter box's top down hard, and dashing to the house, fumbling for keys, hurriedly shoving one into the screen door, and swinging it open with too much force, causing a clang against the red brick.

"Sorry Mum! Just me!" He calls into the house, trying to kick off his shoes, and falling over his own feet to rush into the kitchen. "But look! Mum!"

"Sayang! Ya, hello!" Lydia replies, standing up from her work at the table, and welcoming her son with a warm hug.

"Mum! Look!" Matthew repeats, handing her the envelope, beaming.

"What's this? Your HSC?" She asks, reaching for a butter knife on the table.

"No, Mum, that comes next week." He clarifies, gesturing to the letter, bouncing on the balls of his feet. "This is better."

"I'm sure it's wonderful, Sayang." She affirms, pulling the butter knife through the envelope, and reaching in between the paper. "Oh, what did you get me?"

She playfully shimmies, as Matthew bounces, a small and pure display of shared joy.

"It's... well, just look at it."

Lydia nodding, pulling the contents out, unfolding, and looking over the certificate.

"No..." She says, hand moving to her mouth, eyes on Matthew, tears welling in the corners. "My baby..."

"Yeah, yeah." Matthew affirms, opening his arms, ready for another hug.

Lydia leaning into his embrace, his chin sitting easily on her head, so much bigger now, despite barely being eighteen. Hands gentle and caring, surrounding her smaller frame, excited, but settled.

"My baby..." She repeats, the sound muffling into Matthew's t-shirt. "My sweet baby."

"I am." Matthew replies, voice cracking with tears of his own. "I always will be."

Lydia closing her eyes, soaking in the love of her son, the gesture, the intention, the silent effort in the shadows, but most of all, the peace.

A quiet, breezy, afternoon, just like any other over these past years, loving, simple, peaceful.

"Show me? I didn't get to see it." Matthew asks, rubbing Lydia's shoulders before stepping back.

Lydia handing the certificate silently, wiping a few stray streams, glancing up at her towering son, bringing a hand up to cup his cheek, looking deep into the same eyes she sees in the mirror.

"My baby, Sayang." She repeats, drying one of his tears with her thumb.

"Of course, Mum." Matthew beams through tiny streams, bringing a hand up to cover hers.

A love shared, known, freely given and openly received. Reciprocated, appreciated, wanted.

Lydia nodding, taking her hand down, reaching for a tissue from the box on the document-laden table.

Matthew keeping his own fingers on his cheek, holding up the certificate, taking it in for the first time. There it is.

Matthew William Fletcher Seng.

That's him. That's who he is now. He is his mother's son. On paper. With ink. Official and acknowledged.

It's all he's ever wanted. To walk into a room, to announce to others, to one day have a poem, or a play, or even a film, with that name written all over it.

To be able to bring it back to Lydia Seng herself, and show her the legacy that he's only ever hoped to carry with him.

Fresh tears pooling as he feels Lydia tapping his forearm with a fresh tissue.

He takes it, dabbing his face, watching his mother do the same, then hold her hand out.

"Thank you." He says, placing the used tissue in her palm, watching her walk to the bin. "For everything, Mum."

"Sayang, no- you don't…" She waves, pushing aside his words of adoration.

"But I want to… Mum, please." Matthew pleads, stepping towards his mother. "Can I just say thank you?"

Lydia is defenceless against those big, onyx eyes, waving her son into another hug, this time able to wrap her arms around him too. Feeling safe, feeling home.

"I just want to say…" Matthew continues, turning his head to lay his cheek on the crown of her head. "Thank you for everything. You've been… strong, like, in a way

I can't even imagine, and I don't know... how you did it."

"Oh, Sayang..." She mumbles, words of dismissal, words of affection, words of acceptance.

"I just... I love you so much. You're the reason I am anyone or anything." He continues, voice crumbling under the weight of pure emotion, but not concerning himself with any attempt to hold that truth back. "And I'm gonna try everyday... to show you how much I love you."

"My baby... I love you. And you make it so easy." She insists, burying her head deeper into her son's chest. "But I would do it if it was hard."

A short moment. A silence of comfort. A shared breath.

And then. Lydia laughing. Brash and natural. Bold and unafraid.

Matthew joining. First a chuckle. Then a cackle. Then a bottomless squawk.

A true expression in the safety of a true home.

# Australia Go-Set National Top 40

# Weekly Chart

# 20 March 1971

# No. 12

A light from Matthew's phone, getting Jesse's attention, as it creates a tiny glow on the small table where it was left behind, in favour of rough wrestles, sweet kisses, and even sweeter beverages.

"A notif or something, you wanna get it?" He asks, pointing to the phone, ever the gracious host.

"Oh shit! Daniel!" Matthew bounces up, turning and darting over to his phone swiftly. "Is it ok if I go have a quick call with him? He likes to check up on me."

"Nothing would be more okay ever." He smiles.

Jesse watching a feverishly clicking Matthew, enjoying the shapes of his face as they're lit up by the phone, hair draping down either side, cheeks flushing carmine in his hurry.

Beauty from the comfort of his armchair, a rare treat.

Matthew gesturing to his right, assuming the only door he's seen in this studio apartment is the bathroom, and asking silently if he can take his call in there.

A thumbs up from a sipping Jesse, and a cough as he attempts to cut his sip short.

And he's gone. And Jesse hears the door click softly behind him. Remembering exactly why he doesn't like loud noises.

"May-may, are you okay?" A concerned voice comes through.

"Hey, sorry. You're never gonna guess what happened!" Matthew greets, rushing and enthusiastic. "Jesse, like Jesse from down the street, like Oliveira Nunes, that Jesse. He came to the play tonight, and I'm at his place right now."

"What?" Daniel blurts, baffled, but no less alarmed. "Are you sure it's him?"

"Who else would it be?" Matthew returns, knowing why Daniel is perpetually ready to fight for his safety, but wishing for a little more excitement in this particular moment. "Who else calls me 'May'?"

"I just... wow." Daniel concedes, letting it all sink in. "Are you two ok... is everything... cool?"

"We did pash if that's what you're asking." Matthew beams, ever the younger sibling.

"I wasn't, but... congratulations, I guess." Daniel switches gears, a baffled chuckle coming out, before continuing. "This is... sudden."

"Yeah, yeah... it's kinda nuts." Matthew muses, tracing a finger along the grout between the seashell tiles, mind zipping back and forth all the while. "Like, what are the chances?"

"True, true." Daniel agrees, then realising his duties aren't finished. "I mean... can I... say hi real quick?"

Jesse looking around his apartment, happy he tidied up before he left for the play, the smallest shred of his being having wished he would be back here with May.

Lost in his thoughts, he's unable to hear the voice barely coming through the walls, or a click of the handle, or footsteps towards him. Only looking up when May is in his line of sight.

"Hey, uh... Jay?" Matthew asks, having appeared in the main area of this studio. "Is it cool if Daniel says hi?"

"To me? Yeah!" Jesse eagerly replies, taking the phone. "Whoa, hey! How are you?"

"Oh, it really is you." Daniel's voice comes through, bringing up a face in Jesse's mind, but the years would've changed it. "You sound different, but... the same."

"You sound the same but different." Jesse jokes, smiling up to Matthew. "You all good?"

"Yeah, yeah... I'm- I'm all good, man." Daniel replies, his voice full of a mix of pleasant surprise and confused wistfulness. "Wow, this is… I mean, it's great, but… how'd you…? I don't mean to be rude, but."

"Nah, not rude, mate, all good." Jesse replies, reverting to his Dude Voice, the phrases coming out smooth but feeling slightly foreign. "Yeah, I just… looked May up and… went to the play, and… we're having some lychee fizzies right now."

He gives a little wink to a waiting Matthew, who's towering over, but hands clasped in front, and hunching somewhat, trying to make up for that towering, no doubt.

"Oh… yeah, cool." Daniel replies, the protective lilt coming through loud and clear to Jesse, eldest boy recognising eldest boy. "'Cause May doesn't really drink, so… I mean alcohol, so…"

"Yeah, I guessed." Jesse reassures, aiming for soothing, and perhaps overshooting into just a little dismissive, jumping to explain further. "Me too. I like a clear head when I wreck my shit."

"Yeah, alright." Daniel laughs, tone shifting from less protective to more light-hearted. "Well, I better let ya go, put May-may back on would ya?"

Jesse giving a small sound of agreement, looking up to Matthew, and holding the phone out, nodding encouragingly, happy to take the win.

"Yep?" Matthew answers, listening to Daniel, but with eyes full of Jesse. "Pretty great, right?"

"Yeah." Daniel agrees, hesitating for a moment, before asking the obvious. "You gonna be like... safe and everything?"

'Day-day." Matthew warns, brow furrowing as he feels both looked after and talked down to.

"Sorry, I just... I don't know, I was worried 'cause I hadn't heard from you, and now I'm like..." Daniel stumbles, realising the layers to his simple question too late, hoping to repair the damage with rushed words. "Yeah, sorry, it's hard to turn the Big Brother Switch off."

Matthew smiling softly, sharing a brief look with Jesse, giving a sound of agreement to Daniel.

"Thank you for checking in." He says, sticking to the facts, an air of childish defensiveness colouring his words. "I am fine. I am safe. The preview went well."

"Okay, good." Daniel agrees, before thinking a little levity couldn't hurt. "Well... use lube I guess."

"Thank you, I **did** need my straight brother to tell me that." Matthew jokes, pointing to the phone with a look of wide-eyed disbelief, sharing a glance with Jesse.

He tucks lips in, trying to hold in a laugh, not sure what the other side of the conversation is, but piecing enough together to know it must've been rich.

"Hey, I kissed a nonbinary on the weekend I'll have you know." Daniel retorts, his voice light and a little playful.

"That's a Monday for me." Matthew sarcastically replies.

"Love you, mate." Daniel concedes, suddenly shifting to an absoluteness. "Text me tomorrow?"

"Love you too, will do." Matthew smiles, appreciating the care and support, not in spite of, but because of, it's imperfection. "Thanks for the check-in."

"Anytime. Loveyabye!" Daniel chirps.

Matthew smiling, holding the phone a few inches from his face, calling a mirrored response, finger hovering above the 'End Call' button, then pressing.

Looking to Jesse, he blinks his disbelief into the apartment.

Jesse's laugh finally bursting through, knowing the fill-in is going to be good.

# ARIA Top 50 Albums

# Weekly Chart

# 3 May 2010

# No. 50 (Track 4)

"Also, I have a little brother." Jesse explains, fingers dancing through May's jet black hair. "Alex came out."

Matthew taking a beat to hear Jesse's words, connecting a toddler to 'Alex', trying and failing to open his eyes long enough to look up to Jesse, the strong rays of the November sun making it quite the task.

"Oh! Congratulations to him!" Matthew beams, trying to think of a three-year-old as an adult, before realising he's left out a crucial follow-up. "Him? Or like 'he/they', or... 'they/them' or...?"

"Yeah, they're doing a 'he/they' thing." Jesse nods, smiling sweetly at the squinting Matthew in his lap.

"A 'he/they' thing?" Matthew jumps in, wit sharpening his words. "Isn't that like... wearing a muscle tee and doc martins to a formal event?"

"You're rotten." Jesse jokes, giving Matthew a faux-punch to the stomach, complete with sound effect. "But Alex would love that. I'll text him."

Matthew bringing a hand up to shield himself, as he watches Jesse typing away, those soft features and salmon lips stretching into a glowing smile.

Such ease wafting into Matthew's soul, only as he takes a pause, has a moment to realise it, does it truly come into focus. Jesse simply fills him, not because he's half of a whole, but because being in Jesse's presence is exceptionally uncomplicated.

An absence of pretence or self-censoring, a reality void of worry and scrutiny and invisible confrontations. There's no battle for dominance, no waiting for a moment to strike, or ready to shield, and no talking around and around until words have no meaning. No, this is an overarching sensation of peace.

"Nice. We'll see if they get back to me." Jesse proclaims, sitting down his phone, as his words row into Matthew's thoughts.

"Yeah." Matthew blinks, taking a moment to return to his body, and this park, on a sleepy Wednesday, sitting up as he continues. "And hey, good on your parents, two queer kids out of three, not bad."

Jesse laughs, the cackle exploding out of him, barrelling into the trees, the flowers, the shrubs, beautiful in it's boldness.

He catches himself, hand over mouth, he doesn't usually let his laugh come out so true, so boisterous, he's heard too many complaints, some barely detectable, others downright bold, that it's not a sound people want to hear.

So chuckles subside behind a clutching hand, trying to muffle joy itself.

"It'd be great to get a clean sweep, but." Matthew continues, resting hands on Jesse's forearms, hoping to remove those hands, and hear more of that rushing sound.

Palms smacking black jeans, loud, echoing, delightful laughter filling their corner of the park, Jesse forgetting to keep it down, and simply letting go, here with Matthew.

"No, no, no!" Jesse protests, reaching for Matthew in turn, trying to get the words out between cackles and rushed breaths. "You- you... don't!"

"Mmm? Additional lore?" Matthew questions, joyous smile spreading across his face, hands grasping Jesse's wrists, wanting against everything to keep this going.

Jesse tries, he pushes, he keeps trying, but it's taking a moment, between bleats and breaths, there's barely enough space to explain. And the attempts only fuel the laughter fire.

Matthew watching and squeezing, savouring such simple connection, a richness, a gentleness, like they're still kids, like nothing bad has ever, and will ever, happen.

But of course, the terror was always sewn into Matthew's seams.

And Jesse's was stitched in later.

"No, no... no!" Jesse finally manages, gasping for breath and shaking monkey-gripped arms back and forth, rocking both he and Matthew. "They did get... all three! We're all... little queer deviants!"

A call escapes Matthew's lips, a shout, a scream, but of delight, like a single note in a symphony. And he pulls Jesse in by the grip, his entire body tightening, like a squeaky toy being completely flattened, squeezed until the walls meet.

Jesse pulling back, a joyous tug-of-war, as he bounces in place, boisterous squawks barrelling out from his wheezing chest.

"Tabitha's bi... and poly!" Jesse shouts, becoming louder, running out of breath, voice mixing with Matthew's. "And-and... she runs a nursery!"

Another shout, fast and intense, fireworks shooting from Matthew to Jesse, hitting his face, relishing in the noise, wanting so deeply to be loud together.

Such a small and important freedom, especially for Jesse, told he was doing too much all too often.

God forbid men show happiness.

"She does!" He continues, rocking back and forth, Matthew leading him. "We don't stand... for-for bi-erasure 'round these parts!"

A new note, higher and more intense, rushing over Jesse like rain breaking a heatwave, opening his face completely, a silent scream of joy painted over bronze tones.

"I assumed heterosexuality!" Matthew jokes, loud and high enough to dry paint.

"A fate worse than death!" Jesse volleys, pushing out, low and sarcastic.

Chuckles settle to giggles, and turn to murmurs, like a flower closing as the dusk settles in.

Hands still clasped, but grip loosening slowly, heads turning, glances flitting, from lips, to eyes, and back.

A pause, silent and intense, heavy and urgent.

Collision, rushing and wanting, tasting ferociously. Screaming silently, deep into the unknown, and hearing a love song echoing back.

Hands ferocious, pulling in closer, deeper, grasping at shoulders and necks and waists, rushing and intense, melting into a kiss that tastes of the lifetime apart, and the unspent energy that built up in their bodies during those years.

# Church by American Rock Band

# Fall Out Boy

Tongues tasting, hands busy, thighs pressing, hips grinding. Heavy and vicious and wild. Youthful and wise and misguided.

Kisses along Jesse's jaw, and down his neck, reigniting such hot fire within him, as Matthew's fingers reach for the button of his black jeans.

Hot moans falling from salmon lips, hips lifting in anticipation.

"Please… please, please…" Jesse begs, as he feels the button pop open.

Fly unzipping, hand slipping inside briefs, grasping at Jesse's hard cock, thumb circling the slick tip.

A shuddering whimper rushing out of Jesse, the sensation long overdue, and still taking him by surprise.

"Fuck, fu… ahhh…" He breathes, hands making tight fists above his head, temple rocking to Matthew's, wanting to feel closer. "S-slower… I'm already…"

"Already?" Matthew teases, lifting lips just long enough to speak, then blowing cool air on the trail his kisses left, before continuing. "Someone's overexcited."

"Mmm…" Jesse agrees, body on fire, release creeping up. "I-I… it's y-you…"

"What a compliment." Matthew breathes, grinding his own cock against Jesse's thigh, in time with his strokes of Jesse. "I like when good boys cum for me."

Jesse can only whimper into his apartment. Back and hips and hands to the champagne carpet, glued by his own desire, his own fast-approaching release, crawling through his form, taking over his muscles, his vessels, his blood.

And then two words push their way through the powerful rush.

"..ruin it…" He urges, eyes shutting violently, body pulling taunt, a string on the verge of snapping.

"Oh?" Matthew teases, slowing his strokes and hips, half to be sure, and half to draw this delectable moment all the way out. "What do you say when you want something?"

Jesse can feel it, rising up inside him, so close he can taste it on his lips.

"P-please… ruin it…" He breathes, riding the edge hard. "P_ease… I want to be… good…"

"Then cum, slut." Matthew instructs, deep and commanding, pumping hard. "Shoot into your pants like a good little faggot."

Hips bucking up hard. Cock throbbing fast. Spilling into his briefs.

One good pump. Then it's gone. Ripped away in a second.

Face crumpling. Body tense. Nothing but Matthew's grip on the base.

A long, pained, drawn-out 'fuck' falling out of his mouth, eyes opening to meet Matthew, face looking down at him with delicious satisfaction.

"That's a good boy." Matthew praises, low and soothing, watching Jesse try to catch his breath, looking back at him with white-hot devotion. "Very good."

"Th-thank you…" Jesse stammers, arousal doubled, his wet cock in Matthew's grasp. "Th-"

Words cut off as fingers trace along his shaft, teasing the stimulation he was denied, over-sensitive now, burning under the tiniest touches.

"Good boys clean up too." Matthew instructs, fingers pinching at the tip.

Jesse sharply inhaling in response, barely hearing Matthew's words, before salty fingers are above his lips.

Taking them in hungrily, tasting himself, eyes on Matthew, wanting to give a good preview.

Jesse looks incredible. Sex incarnate. Devoted and undone. Matthew's cock twitching in his pants, wishing to be his slick fingers.

"Oh, fuck." He praises, hips grinding against Jesse's thigh. "You wanna show me more?"

Eyes lighting up. Brow furrowing in arousal. Only pulling back long enough to speak two words.

"Yes please."

Matthew taking his fingers away, a short moan from Jesse, absolutely gone to the moment, beautiful and unravelled.

Wet fingers gripping either side of Jesse's hot face, tight enough for cheeks to dig into teeth, dominant and rough, angling him up, and drawing him into a ferocious kiss.

Fast and deep, Matthew leading and Jesse following, charged and so very new. Wanting to drink in everything, tasting and biting and sucking, a futile attempt to make up for lost time.

Matthew pulling back, holding them both for a beat, looking over Jesse, taking in the glorious sight.

Cheeks flushing magenta, eyes half-closed in a thick daze, breath rushing through him fast and hot. Divine and heavenly.

Giving a soft slap, he relinquishes his grip, moving to stand, tucking a finger inside his waistband, looking at Jesse, ready to fuck that glorious face.

Jesse scrambling to his knees, aching to have that cock in his mouth, dripping with desperation to please Matthew. Hands settling on thighs, walnut eyes looking up to the onyx abyss, wanting to fall through space together.

Fingers walking over to a top button, and popping it free, then gripping a zipper and pulling it down with slow intensity, gaze never leaving Jesse's desperate face.

Jesse arching his back, feeling the wet spot in his briefs make contact with his dick, softening and neglected, just as he craves.

Fingers pulling a hard shaft free, and dark eyes looking down at the inviting sight that is Jesse's salmon lips.

"You want this?" Matthew asks, ready to feel the tip at the back of Jesse's throat.

With eyes fluttering, and mouth hungry, Jesse nods, small and urgent.

Strong hands reaching to clasp an eager face, Jesse letting out a moan at the touch.

Tongue out, mouth wide, eyes burning into Matthew.

Tip making contact, slick and relieving, hands guiding, tentative but charged.

Mouth devouring, wanting and salacious, starving for more.

Slow and controlled, Matthew's breath hitching, warm and pleasurable.

Fingers coming up, gripping into thighs, willing him deeper.

Matthew hearing, easing in further, hitting the very back, soft and hot.

The warm, slick, inviting mouth devouring him hungrily, Jesse presenting submission to him, not something he takes, but something he is freely given, another layer to pleasure, heightening an already delicious thrill.

Keen, salmon lips at the base, making contact with short hairs, nose against skin, engulfing completely.

A hold. Just a beat. A chance to take a snapshot.

And he's moving, with hands surrounding Jesse's skull, and hot moans falling from his lips, Matthew thrusting slowly, not wanting to rush, needing to absorb every sensation into every cell of his body.

Eyes closing, so Jesse can drop completely into his frame, savouring the feeling. He's just a head, he's here to be used, he's a tool for another, and that other is Matthew, finally.

Whimpers vibrating through his body, spent and unsatisfied cock tingling in his pants, hips moving with Matthew's, lewd and salacious.

And fiery with arousal, punctuated by thrusts, Matthew speaks:

"Still. A. Horny. Slut?" He teases, pressing fingers deeper into Jesse's face and hair, pace increasing as he continues. "Can. You. Take. More?"

A muffled 'mhmm' radiates around Matthew's cock, as he watches it disappear into Jesse's mouth again, the sensation causing his head to tilt back, glorious and righteous, inching his release closer.

He bucks all the way down, holding Jesse while he asks:

"You gonna make this dick cum, faggot?"

Deep and gruff, a voice Jesse never imagined could come from Matthew.

And with his mouth full of cock and his skull surrounded by tight grip, a searing flash of arousal jolts through him, his own dick twitching in his soaked briefs.

Matthew pulling him off just as quick, looking down at him, waiting for an answer.

But he's floaty, he's gone, he's drifting along a glorious plane between this world and the next, dancing on a tightrope between heaven and purgatory, words can't find him here.

Nodding, enthusiastic and desperate, with eyes half-closed and grip loosening on thighs. A sight delicious and lewd enough to have Matthew spilling untouched onto those slick lips and flushed cheeks.

Releasing one hand slowly, Matthew traces light touches from Jesse's dark curls, across glistening face, over plumped lips, and to his slick cock, stroking lazily.

"You want it on your face or down your throat, slut?" He asks, looking down at a worshipping Jesse, watching him with a devotion of divinity. "Your choice."

With hips winding, eyes struggling to focus, sweat shining all over, and mouth empty, Jesse tries to catch his words.

But they evade him.

And all he can manage is to open his mouth as wide as possible, and press his tongue past his dripping lower lip, hoping it's a sufficient answer.

Matthew gliding the tip of his cock over Jesse's top lip teasingly, as he watches Jesse's eyes try to follow, before pulling a confirmation out of the melted man on his knees.

"Throat?"

Simple and clear.

Jesse trying to manage a nod, with brow furrowing in arousal, and saliva continuing to leak down his lips, and over his chin, hoping he's being clear enough.

Fingers moving from shaft to cheek, and up into dark curls, gripping firm again, relishing in the salacious sight of Jesse so desperate to please him.

Matthew guiding slowly, all the way down, letting out a thick moan as he hits the back of Jesse's throat, taking in a shaky breath, feeling an almighty pulse rush through him, urgent and fervent.

Watching Jesse's eyes close again, he pulls back and bucks forward, faster this time, chasing that approaching ecstasy.

Again. And again. Harder and faster as he moves. It's right there. Glorious and close. Moans and hot breath rushing out. Eyes slamming shut. Muscles tensing.

A string of 'ah, fuck' falling from blush lips, and he looks down to Jesse once more, as he thrusts one last time.

Release rushing over him, short bucks shaking his hips, breath escaping him in a loud, ardent, moan.

Floating through time and space, body light and free, encased in rapture. Flying, dying, slipping between dimensions for a split second that stretches the glorious moment into an age.

Pulsing and throbbing as euphoria floods over him, he looks down, his cock buried in Jesse's mouth, those hands around his thighs, that back arched for his enjoyment, those eyes closed in focus, it's a sight that sends one last pulse through him, and a final, shuddering, moan past blush lips.

Jesse lost in the sensation, the overwhelm of the stress on his spine, the pressure on his knees, the tingle in his gripping fingers, the throbbing cock hitting the very back of his throat, the hot spill down his oesophagus, and the aching, unpleasured, cock in his jeans. It's a combination that has him feeling a spectacular, moreish, luscious mix of sensations.

Slowly, with thrusts that grow shallower, Matthew pulls back from Jesse, the last few drops hitting his tongue on the way out, allowing for a chance to taste the man he's often dreamt of being used by.

Fingers playing in Jesse's dark curls, thumbs coming up to stroke over his forehead, feeling the slick of sweat on his brow, and the fire under his skin.

Matthew kneeling down to his level, looking him over, unseen by closed walnut eyes, as fingers trace over magenta cheeks, that strong nose, and those wet, salmon, lips, running a thumb over the mix of fluids.

Jesse opening his mouth lazily, unsure of his expected response from Matthew, and not really in any state to think that far ahead, just wanting a little more of something, anything.

Matthew answering with a slow, deep, intimate kiss, tasting himself on Jesse's lips and tongue, feeling the slick on that chin, those cheeks, and as his hands explore around, on the back of that neck.

Jesse, dedicated and unravelled in his hands, on his lips, under his spell, beautiful and devilish.

Excerpt from:

# MY HAND

# IN YOURS

Written & Directed

By

Matthew Seng

# SCENE FOUR
# DRINKS AT HIS PLACE

**lounge room, sofa stage left, armchair centre stage, small coffee table between**

*JACOB is sitting on the sofa*

**FADE UP – Pink Wash**
**FADE UP – Audio Track 2 – 'Radio'**

*MICHAEL enters, carrying two drinks*

MICHAEL
[uneasy, stumbling]
So, hey… thanks for…
I dunno… getting it…

*MICHAEL holds one drink out for JACOB*

*JACOB takes the drink with a reassuring nod*

JACOB

[clear, even]

Getting... your sexuality?


*MICHAEL sits on the arm of the armchair. He's tense*


MICHAEL

[uneasy]

Um... yeah?


JACOB

[genuine]

What is there to get?


MICHAEL

[confessing, a little ashamed]

For some people... a lot


JACOB

[with love]

That's shit.

And those people are missing out.

*MICHAEL smiles softly, uneasy and pushing,
eyes low*

JACOB (cntd.)

[playful, loving]

And like,

you are attracted to men...

*MICHAEL relaxing, easy in the change to banter*

MICHAEL

[playful, bantering]

I'm following, tell me more...

JACOB

[bantering]

And I, I don't know

if you know this,

but I, am a men.

MICHAEL

[bantering]

Wait... you are?

JACOB

[bantering]

Yep, just a little

something about me.


MICHAEL

[bantering]

So interesting.


JACOB

[bantering]

Thank you.

And so if you're

attracted to men,

and I'm a men,

what else is there to consider?


MICHAEL

[bantering, pointing]

That's a water-tight argument


*MICHAEL smiles truly, it fills his entire face*

MICHAEL

[relaxing, genuine]

But seriously…

thank you for saying that.


JACOB

[soft, caring]

Well, I mean it, so…


*MICHAEL holds up his drink*


MICHAEL

[light, relaxed]

I'll drink to that.


*JACOB holds up his drink*


JACOB

[caring, playful]

To the bisexuals.

MICHAEL

[receptive, playful]

To the bisexuals!


*MICHAEL and JACOB take a sip of their drinks*


**FADE OUT – Pink Wash**

**FADE OUT – Audio Track 2 – 'Radio'**

Kent Music Report

National Top 100 Singles

Year End Chart

1985

No.70

"Fuck…" Jesse sighs, tossing the used tissues towards the bin, and missing.

"Mmm…" Matthew agrees, looking over Jay's flushed body, glistening in the harsh, early-evening sunlight of late December. "Your elbows okay? You didn't safeword, so…"

"Nah yeah, of course not." Jesse dismisses, slinging a thigh over Matthew's hip, and letting his head flop onto the damp pillow. "Come on, I *would* safeword if it was more than I could handle."

Matthew giving a sound of acknowledgement, smiling softly in the afterglow, right hand finding Jesse's left thigh, enjoying the casual intimacy of a leg over his own.

"So are we gonna talk about the 'GOOD BOY' tattoo or, like…?" Matthew asks, fingers tracing the ink a palm's distance from the delicious crease in Jesse's hip, gaze fixed on the two words, mind wandering. "...just pretend it's not there?"

"What is there to say?" Jesse teases, eyes never leaving Matthew's face, completely enamoured. "I want to be."

"A good boy..." He muses, inky eyes returning to Jesse, looking over the magenta flush still evident under those gorgeous bronze tones. "I think you're an alright boy."

"How can you say that?" Jesse shoots back, voice barely able to commit to much above unravelled and exhausted. "I'll suck your dick again right now."

"You sure you'll be able to manage?" Matthew pushes, left thumb coming up to trace along Jesse's bottom lip. "Not too tired?"

"You sure *you* can manage?" Jesse volleys, trying to push through the haze of sex, heavy in his mind, floating all around his naked body, sinking him into the mattress. "Your dick can go a third time? 'Cause my mouth sure can."

He takes Matthew's thumb into his mouth, giving it the same affection he showed on his knees not an hour ago.

"Hey, hey, hey..." Matthew repeats, pulling his thumb back, Jesse letting go easily. "Is this like a 'I wanna fuck again' thing or a 'I wanna avoid this topic' thing?"

"Por que no los dos?" He jokes, shrugging, looking up to the ceiling.

"Jesse." May gently pushes, kind in a way that might not be heard as such.

No reply. A retreat. Walnut eyes falling. Words failing to come to the lips. Stuck in the mind.

"Jesse?" May tries again, concern coming through more thoroughly.

It's heard. Unsticking the words.

"I'm... I don't wanna be all talking about exes..." Jesse answers, gaze locked on the words between May's casual fingers.

"I mean... I know you've been fucking..." Matthew states, the tiniest amount of humour bubbling up, and he rids it from his mouth, as he continues. "And I know you're bi, if this is about... someone who's not a man?"

A fast silence, rushing in like a cold southerly in the middle of a boiling night, but this chill isn't wanted.

"Clove did it." He speaks, warming the air.

"Okay... who's Clove?" Matthew leads, trying to ease the words out without pushing too hard.

"She's... she *was* my boss..." Jesse answers, eyes busy, unfocusing, seeing only a blur of skin, memories rushing back. "Who was fucking me."

"…I mean… it's the arts, that happens. A lot." Matthew replies, matter-of-fact as you like, as though this is as mundane as small talk at the bus stop. "I would know."

"Yeah, I guess so." Jesse agrees, hoping to close this off sooner rather than later. "Long story short: it's a stick and poke she gave me one fuck-getaway and I'm… I dunno… it still, like… has her ghost or something."

"Right. Okay." Matthew nods, fingers retreating from Jesse's thigh.

"Are you… freaked out about that?" Jesse asks, eyes snapping to the movement, worry flooding him that such a simple gesture could be loaded with meaning.

"Not really." May answers, settling the back of that same hand on Jesse's middle, not wanting to keep touch on a haunted spot.

"No?" Jesse asks, bringing a finger to May's open palm, drawing circles, light and tender.

"There's not much to be freaked out about." May shrugs, watching the circles warmly. "Jesse, I've been fucking and sucking and snorting ket with the best of them. You think I care that this tiny part of your body is still tied to someone you were fucking what, a year ago?"

"Three years ago." Jesse rushes in, the sounds leaving his mouth before he can think to hold them back.

"Oh."

The one syllable comes out low. Jesse feels that rush again.

"You *are* freaked out." He deflates, voice soft and hurt, his circles halting.

"No, no…" Matthew explains, closing his hand, holding Jesse's finger. "I'm just… processing."

"I hadn't fucked anyone since her…" Jesse spills, his lips moving fast again, too quick to be stopped. "…and she… got under my skin. Oh-" He pauses, realising the double-meaning, a small scoff coming out. "In that way too."

"Okay, yep." Matthew nods, opening his palm, this time to let Jesse's hand settle into his. "I can get that."

"Are you sure?" Jesse asks, interlacing fingers, sliding into Matthew.

"I mean… I don't think I've ever…" May muses, eyes fixed on joined hands. "…been hung up on anyone but you, so…"

"Well, I was hung up on you the whole fucking time." Jesse half-jokes, truth looping along every second stitch of his words. "If that's any consolation."

"It'll have to do for now." Matthew replies, giving a sleepy nudge from his shoulder to Jesse's.

A single, bubbling, light-as-air 'thanks' tumbling out of Jesse as he rolls back into place. The small shove welcomed, a reminder he's still a joyous kid, somewhere inside.

"Are you... okay though?" Matthew asks, seeing Jesse fade away. "Do you wanna talk more about Clove?"

Jesse flits his gaze to onyx eyes, falling into the warm, dense, ether.

"That wouldn't be weird?" He asks, lost in the welcoming black.

"I mean, I'm not like, an expert at romantic relationships, but I'm pretty sure being a friend is also part of it." May answers, humour carrying his words, lightening the load. "And if this is like a friend matter, then I want to listen."

"Oh."

The single sound is all Jesse can manage, unable to look into May, his eyes fall, lost in thought instead.

He can feel every romantic relationship flick through his mind, a Rolodex of moments, pauses, contemplations, eyes looking away. Words thought and never spoken, words spoken and never heard, words heard and never understood.

And what if they had? Maybe there was something like this waiting for him in all those hook-ups, fuckbuddies, and secret rendezvous. Something he was never willing or able to see, never feeling safe enough to just speak, and so holding his peace, until it ate him up inside, becoming his war instead.

"Jay?" Matthew probes gently, running loving fingers through dark brown curls. "Anyone home?"

Jesse breathing to attention, touches in his hair, hand holding his, mind coming back to May, gaze coming back to the fading blush of carmine, almost gone from glowing almond skin, the sexuality leaving this moment in more ways than one.

"Yeah, I'm home." Jesse smiles, meaning more than the words' face value.

"Me too." May agrees, seeing Jesse's double meaning in those big eyes. "And I'm here for you."

A sudden air of bashfulness taking over Jesse, as his gaze moves to Matthew's bare chest instead, bringing right hand up to draw circles over the sparce, fine, hair, busying his fingers to distract his racing mind.

"So... Clove?"

"It's... kind of a long story..." Jesse brushes, so used to pushing and ignoring.

"Well, I don't have anywhere to be, so I think I can fit this in." He volleys, a small chuckle following his words.

Jesse joining a beat later, his laugh even tinier.

"Alright, well..." He reaches, trying to line his words up, hoping for something closer to a picket fence, rather than a dominoes run, ready to topple. "I'm basically freelance, but I did have a contract with this particular touring company for a while... and that's where Clove worked."

Matthew watching Jesse's lips create the words, listening to every syllable with intention, wanting to understand every corner of this man's brain, being, and blood.

"And, yeah... it was... sort of a game of chicken for a while." Jesse recalls, pictures of sultry glances, words with hidden meaning, and plausible deniability touches, racing through his mind. "Like, how far can we go before one of us says something?"

"That's... kind of hot." Matthew muses, compersion wafting over him, the idea of Jesse being teased by a mystery woman suddenly enticing.

"It was." Jesse smiles, catching a twinkle in May's eye. "I ended up wanking in the toilets at work more than once."

"Oh shit." Matthew teases, imagining a desperate, rushing, Jesse, getting off on company time. "What are you, a teenager?"

He was. Charged up then like he'd been years before. Like he is now. Maybe he'll always be. Seasons come and pass, but he remains undimmed by time.

"I kinda felt like one." He muses, recalling hotel rooms in foreign countries. "I even came by, like... humping the mattress, like, all the time. It became our thing."

"She... told you to do that?" Matthew probes, excited by the idea of such a worked-up, sexually-charged Jesse, humping a mattress like a possessed being.

"No, like... while I was going down on her, and then I'd be like so worked up that, like..." Jesse elaborates, knives on his skin, hands on his shoulders, and his blood on her lips, all rattling around his head. "Just a little grinding and I'm cumming."

"And here I have to fuck you." Matthew jokes, a lazy hand closing around a tuff of Jesse's curls.

"And I thank you for your service." Jesse throws back, feeling the soft grab, a mirror of the aggression from earlier.

"As you should." Matthew volleys, releasing the soft grasp of one hand, and stroking thumb over knuckles with the other. "It's fucking hard yakka."

"Absolutely awful for you." Jesse laughs, eyes watching fingers, but mind seeing Matthew above him, moaning deep and gruff. "But yeah, when we finally started actually fucking, me and Clove, we we're doing knife play a lot, which I've always liked, but like, with her... it was... more intense."

"Oh?" Matthew leads, snapping up to Jesse's face, waiting for more.

"Yeah, like… I mean, you can see all the faint scars, see? kinda in between the tatts here, and here." Jesse explains, gliding his left hand between the cactus on his right outer forearm, the ghost on that inner forearm, and compass on that deltoid, tracing over barely visible cuts along the way. "Most of them are almost gone, but like… there's one for every time we fucked, cause I… just had to… she had this, like… intensity to her, and she would like, play with my blood, so…"

Matthew's eyes taking in Jesse's skin, the tatts, the faint marks in between, with fresh, zealous, eyes. Where before he'd seen Jesse's body as a whole, as a beautiful, perfervid, lewd entity, he's now seeing the details, that which must be studied to truly be seen. Only possible when we slow, when we breathe, when we settle.

"Do you… like that?" He asks, looking back to Jesse finally.

'I liked it… with Clove." Jesse answers simply, eyes meeting Matthew's, as he continues with salacious flirtation. "But I'd be open to doing it again… with you."

'Good to know." Matthew smiles, a thought popping into his brain, and he feels he might as well share that too. "I mean… what if… I cut your lip, and kissed you?"

Salmon lips opening, jaw low and slack, walnut eyes wide, he can barely believe it.

"Oh, y-yeah... fuck." Jesse stumbles, the words falling out with little meaning, simply an interjection of sudden, burning, desire.

"Very good to know." Matthew nods slowly, fingers leaving Jesse's hair, tracing down, thumb rubbing over faded scars and ink as he goes. "Let's get the knives out next time. I assume you've got some?"

"Uh huh..." Jesse manages, watching Matthew's touch snake along his skin, hypnotised.

"And what else did you do with Clove?" Matthew leads, down to Jesse's elbow now.

"Yeah, so... um, yeah... knives, flogging, blood..." Jesse recalls, trying to focus while Matthew's hands are on him always being quite the task. "...and bruises, and... break-and-enter rape play..."

Matthew stops at the cactus, surprised by his own interest.

"So... that's you... getting broken into... and... raped?"

Heat rushing Jesse, a delicious mix of arousal and embarrassment. Snippets of Clove's hands pushing him against the champagne carpet, her strap buried deep inside, the soft buzz of her vibe barely audible over the hot groans in his ear.

All he can manage is a small 'mmm'.

"And... would you want me, hypothetically, to break in..." Matthew suggests, fingers dancing from wrist as he speaks, settling on hip, as he continues. "...and fuck you... while you struggle?"

Jesse's mouth doesn't seem to work, he tries to form words, even a single syllable, but he's clouded, his head is in a thousand places, and rushing with flashes. Matthew's hand over his mouth, another pulling down his jeans, and then the cold metal of a knife against his throat.

"Maybe..." Matthew continues, giving a soft squeeze as his hands leaves Jesse's hip, and tracing to sit just inside the armpit. "Nod if that sounds like something... you want to try at some point? We can talk it out further another time."

Jesse nodding vigorously, mouth once again trying for words, and drastically underperforming.

"Noted. I'll keep it up here and ask again at another time." Matthew tilts his head and winks. "And, can I ask... what's it like?" Matthew continues, filling in the space as he watches Jesse come back. "Going down on... well, I guess not a woman, but... yeah, like, eating pussy?"

"Oh, you've never...?"

"Nah. I mean..." Matthew replies, remembering a suave, sweet, sensual, guy named Sam. "I was flirting with this trans guy once, we met at this queer party, and he was a really hot kisser, got his number, texted a bit, but we never ended up getting together, so... but yeah... is that- I just... I'm a little curious. Is it like eating arse or...?"

Jesse absorbs Matthews words for a beat, having never really considered monosexuality outside of his teens, and trying to wrap his head around a style of attraction so different to his own, and yet so similar.

But what he comes up with is much more simple.

"You know what, I've never eaten arse." He speaks, concluding that was the best throughline.

"Never?"

"Nuh, I'm just such a bottom, so..." Jesse muses, recalling different fingers grasping his skull, in all their glorious diverse ways, as he sucked and licked between thighs. "I just like to suck dick and eat pussy, never at the same time, though."

"We should fix that." Matthew smirks, mind wandering to sharing Jesse with someone else, and salacious curiosity of what sides he might see of this man float up in such a moment. "You never eating arse, and me never eating pussy."

"You... want to bring a woman in here?" Jesse asks, surprise lifting his voice more than intended.

"Hey, someone with a pussy." Matthew playfully corrects, giving a quick squeeze of Jesse's bicep. "The person doesn't have to be a woman."

"I can't believe I did a transphobia." Jesse jokingly gasps, wanting to keep the bit going, and stay as long as he can, in a space where even corrections are light and good-natured. "And you caught it. That means you're *better* than me."

"It *really* does." Matthew volleys, before shedding his humour, and finding some truth underneath. "But... I mean, I'm thirty-two years old, call it autistic curiosity, but I can't live my whole life never having sucked a clit."

"Oh, fuck!" Jesse exclaims, pulling his fingers from Matthew's to cover his face with both hands.

"Is that... not how you do it?" Matthew asks, a sharp sting of embarrassment shooting through him.

"I mean... some people like that." Jesse answers, peaking behind fingers to reassure a clearly awkward Matthew. "Clove liked that. She showed me exactly how, by like... demonstrating on her hand, it was really hot."

"Ok, you gotta show me a pic of her." Matthew declares, intrigued enough to put a face to the tales.

"Oh... yeah, let me... grab my..." Jesse speaks, lowering his hands completely, reaching behind him for his phone, and clicking through to a profile he couldn't bring himself to unfollow or block. "There she is." He declares, handing the phone to May.

He's met with a figure with a shaved head, wearing gold-rimmed aviator sunglasses, who's giving the camera two caramel middle fingers, with a wide, devious smile spreading across tawny lips. Adorned with simple gold jewellery – small earing cuffs, a thick bangle, and a gold necklace – she shines through the image, three-dimensional, even in a flat, pixelated, approximation. And the outfit only adds to her appeal. A tangerine blazer without a shirt underneath, so there's just the tiniest hint of the electric blue lace bra peaking through. It's toeing a line of professional and flirty, yet showing off an unerring colour sense.

Matthew looking over the image with admiration. He may not be attracted to women, but he can tell when a woman is attractive. And more so, he gets it. He can see what drew Jesse in.

"Well, fuck." He states, staring at the one and only Clove Venkadeshan. "She's completely gorgeous. And like, the style is... with her colouring... and the shaved head... I mean, wow."

"Don't I know it."

"What are you doing with me, fuck ya?" Matthew quips, handing the phone back.

"You're asking the wrong guy." Jesse jokes back, putting his phone in the top drawer, unimportant once again. "I guess I'm like, in love with you or something."

"Oh."

Like a shot the words barrel through the air. Stillness in it's wake.

Jesse knows, Matthew knows, but it still comes as a shock.

"I didn't... I mean..." Jesse tries, before shaking those ridiculous thoughts from his head. "Actually, fuck it. I do love you, so there. Deal with that. Whatever, fuck ya."

'Wow, that's really embarrassing for you." Matthew teases, smiling wide, dancing fingers into Jesse's palm. "It would be less embarrassing if... I love you too, though. And I do."

A relief. A freedom. A shot of adrenaline to the heart. An affirming, wonderful, gentle landing to an uncertain leap.

Jesse allowing the sensation to wash over him, to turn up the corners of his lips into a full, rich smile. Closer to May now more than ever, speaking truths big and small, feeling heard in so many ways, and being seen in his contentment.

Dark eyes see it, the depth of such comfort, and Matthew takes it in gladly, blessed to see and hear and feel so much of Jay, and like instinct, like nature, eyes closing, just like the small gap between faces.

Jesse leaning into a soft, short, punctuating, kiss.

# ARIA Top 100 Albums

# Year End Chart

# 2009

# No. 61 (Track 11)

Fingers inside, massaging that sweet spot, walls gripping in response.

Eyes watching, revelling in Jesse's face, magenta flushing his cheeks, as he looks up at Matthew, full of pleasure.

Cock hard, pressing against thigh, the small friction providing Matthew some solace in the anticipation.

"Right there?" Matthew asks, laced with desire and a sprinkle of tease.

"Uh-huh..." Jesse whimpers, helpless against Matthew's touch, just as he'd often ached for.

Matthew smiling, dominant and playful, relishing in the sight of Jesse melting under his spell.

Bringing his other hand to trace along Jesse's torso, the skin already dewy, his fingers catching ever so, as he feels the breath rushing those lungs – the reply to his massaging.

And he just wants more.

"Ready for three?" He breathes, hips bucking absentmindedly, cock aching for friction, as his fingers feel it for now.

Jesse only managing a nod.

In the streams of November afternoon sunlight, with salmon lips parted, wanton face glistening, brown eyes fluttering, he's a remarkable sight, and all Matthew can do is watch, finally able to see this side of Jesse. His ultimate Holy Grail.

The urge to slow, to take every second in, to feel this moment in his bones, rushing over Matthew.

His desire for more sensation, for friction, for contact, shifting into a deep ache for tenderness.

Two fingers pulling out gently, a respite from the building sexual tension, from the moving towards an end goal, and a reset, a falling into the now, to more deeply appreciate what is right in front of him.

Instead of replacing with three, he traces fingers from torso, up and over Jesse's thigh, along the hot skin, to the bent knee, and under the fold, feeling the heat in the crease. Onyx locking on walnut, bringing head down, to lay kisses gently on Jesse's knee, around the curve, among the trimmed hair, over old scars. Tender, slow, meaningful.

Jesse watching, his grip on the bed head tightening, as he witnesses the tiny, yet huge, gesture of love, presentness, and sensuality.

He swallows hard, squirming a little, part of him wanting to pull away. Crumbling under the intimacy of the wordless pause, the meaning clear to him, without a sound exchanged.

"...come here... please." He speaks, tiny and desperate, eyes locked on Matthew. "...please..."

Matthew looking over Jesse, knowing this was a different brand of begging, this was nothing to do with play and kink and dynamics.

This is something else, a deep aching need.

Hand gliding from crease, down Jesse's thigh, over his side, and finally up to his shoulder, the other joining, as Matthew moves to hold himself over, taking a beat to breathe Jesse in.

Brown eyes fixing on blush lips, as Jesse can think of nothing else, and has used up his words already.

Closing the gap slowly, wanting to absorb everything this moment has to offer, Matthew moves to lay completely over Jesse, arms tucking under shoulders, chest pressing to chest, hips meeting hips, desire burning between.

Mouths capturing a kiss in a second stretching into oblivion, with no end in sight.

Passionate and chaste at once, bodies melting into each other, as time is no match for the depth of this sensation.

Eventually, lips begin parting, tongues speaking, slow and deep, curious and exploratory, tasting, feeling, exchanging desire back and forth.

Fingers grasping at Jesse's shoulders, sinking into bronze skin, into the ink of the swallow on his left scapula, how it raises the flesh, sitting just underneath, felt only when truly soaking in the contact, and Matthew is absolutely saturated.

Gripping firmly on the bedhead, wanting to remain exposed, vulnerable to every touch, every grab, every sensual movement of Matthew's mouth, seeking surrender and finding salvation.

Swimming, together in a mix of playful youth and sensual wisdom, weightless on Jesse's cheap IKEA bed, like it was a sacred realm, for only May and Jay.

It's Jesse who finally pulls away, head spinning, body aching, hands numb in their grip.

"Please... May..." He breathes, knee coming up, hugging Matthew's waist, hoping he's clear enough. "...please..."

Matthew barely realising how ready he is, the pent-up arousal rushing him at Jesse's words.

"...fuck... look at you..." He mumbles, the words falling out of him.

Eyes fluttering, face burning magenta, glistening with heat, breath thick and hot, rushing Matthew with it's urgency.

"...pl-please..." Jesse manages, undone under Matthew's frame, every cell in his body begging and desperate.

Matthew doesn't need to drag it out of Jesse, he wants to feel that closeness just as urgently, and as he traces touches along Jesse's torso, and sits back on his heels, he sees the wet pool collected on the tip of his purple-hard cock, and the tell-tale spot it left on Jesse's hip. His hand finding the shaft, needing just a little sensation, and stroking so slowly he's barely moving, his release an inch from reach, and his soul hoping that he can at least feel himself inside Jesse first.

Walnut eyes watching jealously, as Jesse's gaze locks on Matthew's hand, imagining that was him, hips rolling without a thought, his want controlling his body, nothing else behind or in front of him, as he falls into the ether.

The other almond hand feverishly patting around the bedsheets, hoping to find the small bottle by feel, and with a pat, then another, it's in Matthew's grasp.

Fingers coating, finding their way inside, rubbing that good spot, watching it take Jesse's breath away.

Back arching, fingers pressing into metal, arms pressing his skull, as the sensation rushes Jesse, like nothing he'd felt before, and intensity reserved for an intimacy like this.

"...j-just go..." Jesse begs, trying to hold his knees up, wanting Matthew all around him.

One hand moving from cock to thigh, up the curve, under the knee, pressing it firmly into Jesse's chest.

A gasp telling Matthew it's more than appreciated.

The other hand easing out, gliding lube over his waiting cock, then lining him up.

Jesse nodding, whimpering, unable to hold back, and no reason to.

Gently, feeling each ridge grip him, Matthew eases inside, watching Jesse as he moves, wanting to remember every second.

A deep, low, moan rumbling out of Jesse, as he feels Matthew pushing in slowly, and finally, hips to hips, connected completely.

"oh... f-fuck..." Jesse moans, breath catching as he feels Matthew pull back a little, and massage that good spot as he moves.

A tingling hand leaving the metal frame, as Jesse reaches for Matthew's face, needing to feel him even closer.

Wide, onyx, eyes, watch Jesse's reaching, surprised to see a new side so soon, and all too happy to comply.

Right hand coming up to steady him, landing by Jesse's compass tattoo, and with the other, Matthew is tracing touches from behind knee, down to thigh, onto hip, along a heaving middle, and up, to settle under Jesse's shoulder.

One last glance of those pleading walnut eyes, and Matthew is capturing Jesse's salmon lips in a deep, passionate kiss – slow, sinking, sensual.

Hips following hips, as tongues taste each other, Jesse folding himself up tightly, under Matthew's form, knees high, squeezed between two sets of shoulders, ankles and heels hooking around Matthew's back, intertwined and connected, almost enough sensation for someone always seeking more.

A tingling hand reaching around to Matthew's neck, fingers in thick, jet black locks, as a few stick to the glistening skin, digits lacing between strands, gentle yet screaming.

Closer, he wants May closer, any gap is simply too far.

Matthew hearing loud and clear, shifting his right hand, leaning down completely, closing any and all space, hooking that hand under Jesse's swallow, fingers dancing over the ink once again, settling almond digits into the raises in Jesse's bronze tones.

Skin on skin, breath expanding, allowing torsos to touch, slick with sweat where they meet.

Lips and tongues and mouths speaking a language of lust and naïveté and ever-aching want.

Hips rolling and grinding, no end and no beginning, smooth and lewd, feeling and sharing and loving.

Jesse drifting fingers from neck, travelling down a hot spine, slow and deliberate, trying to find the source of those strokes.

His other hand joining, finally leaving the metal, tracing from Matthew's elbow, up to scapula, and fingers fanning out on a rolling back.

Digits pressing into Matthew's soft arse, firmer and firmer, following the rolling grind, as the other hand reaches the other cheek, and he's holding onto May with every part of him.

It's enough. It's finally enough. An itch sat untouched for years, finally scratched.

And Jesse never wants to stop scratching.

His mouth leaving May's, gasping for air, moaning into the crook of May's neck, lips resting on slick skin, breath rushing between the tiniest of spaces.

It's cooling, in the heat of such desire, such intense, driving need, and Matthew leans his forehead against the pillow, eyes remaining closed, drifting completely in the torrid everything of this moment.

Jesse's breath on his skin, taste on his lips, knees against his chest, thighs on his belly, hands on his arse, and wanting walls pulsing around his cock, while he's rolling urgent hips deep inside.

He can feel it, he's hitting that good spot, he's hearing from Jesse, the hitch in those moans, and he just knows. And it's all he wants, to make Jesse feel good, for as long as he can.

"...fuck..." Jesse mumbles, teeth against collarbone, hot air rushing around his cry. "...I'm... I'm close..."

May tilting his head, lips to Jesse's neck, laying a wet kiss on glistening skin, trailing his lip up to the lobe, teeth grazing gently against the flesh.

Jay whimpering high against May's skin, his grip on those arsecheeks tightening, willing May to move faster, just a little more.

"...you... you gonna cum... for me?" May asks, voice ragged, thrusts speeding up, his own release a touch away. "...my good... boy?"

The answer comes in a surge of thick, high moans, Jesse's orgasm taking over him, rushing through him, spilling between their chests.

Fingers sinking deep into May's cheeks, ankles pressing together around that back, teeth sinking into shoulder, barely muffling the sultry, loud, mix of whimpers and grunts leaving Jesse's body.

His walls pulsing intense and deep, the sensation rushing his system, bucking his hips wildly, with each rich, hot, throb. Being guided by his own ecstasy, taking over his body, possessing him with thick, satisfying, salvation.

Floating through the pleasure, rescued by the rapture, all body, all gratification, completely on another plane of existence.

Matthew trying to hold off, urging his cock to just fuck, just move, just keep hitting that spot, trying to leave his body long enough to keep Jay riding high in such gracious rescue.

But Jesse has other plans.

"...May..."

The single word rings out like electricity through Matthew's hips, his cock pulsing hard before he even fully comes back to himself, each pulse jolting his thrusts unevenly.

Breath rushing his lungs, grunts falling from his lips, deep into the crook of Jesse's neck. Fingers sinking into Jesse's shoulders, the slick of sweat and cum between their chests, as his own release fills Jesse's squeezing walls.

A duet of pleasure, moans and whimpers and grunts, exchanging back and forth, euphoria filling the room, sinking into Jesse's mattress, interlacing itself in the metal bedframe, settling into the pillows and duvet, blessing this space with the beauty of such intense, human, paradise.

To fly, to soar, to rise up into something unlike the simple humanity of the physical, or the emotional, or the spiritual, but to reach a height only known to the majestic mix of all – and with another, one who was ripped away before either even knew what they were to each other - it's potency sacred and it's height harrowing, yet comfortable, in the here and now, with one so needed, so yearned for, finally found. No longer lost. Not to time or place or to the heart of another. No, found and safe. Finally.

Excerpt from:

# MY HAND

# IN YOURS

Written & Directed

By

Matthew Seng

# SCENE EIGHT
# THE FLOOR OF HIS PLACE

**lounge room, sofa stage left, armchair centre stage, small coffee table between**

*JACOB and MICHAEL are laying on the floor, in front of the coffee table*

*JACOB is facing the audience, propped up on elbows, looking over MICHAEL*

*MICHAEL is facing the ceiling, hands over belly*

**FADE UP – Pink Wash**

**FADE UP – Audio Track 2 – 'Radio'**

JACOB

[genuine, caring]

What's going on in that head?

*MICHAEL chuckles, one of affection*

*JACOB chuckles, one of relief*

*MICHAEL looks to JACOB, a welcoming, loving expression waiting for him*

MICHAEL

[unsure, finding it]

I just... I dunno...

can I ask something

that might... kill the mood?

JACOB

[a little playful]

Now you have to ask

I gotta know what it is.

*MICHAEL awkwardly gets up onto all fours*

*JACOB watching and mirroring, not wanting to make any sudden moves or be left behind*

*MICHAEL crawls over to the sofa, it's childish and raw, and incredibly quiet*

*JACOB following suit, a gesture of deep love*

*MICHAEL and JACOB flop onto the sofa, looking to each other*

*JACOB holds his hand out*

MICHAEL

[more sure, but reserved]

Why did... you stop writing me?

JACOB

[a little lost]

Writing... you?

MICHAEL

[still reserved]

Our letters... we used to...

*JACOB's hand remains out, untaken*

*MICHAEL sees, and does not reach back*

JACOB

[realising]

Oh, yeah... yeah, yeah

we wrote back and forth

for a bit

MICHAEL

[tiny, ashamed]

...a year.

JACOB

[clarifying]

Sorry?

MICHAEL

[hurt]

Almost a year... we wrote...

you don't remember?

*JACOB looks to his hand, then to MICHAEL, he begins to curl his fingers in, the movement catches MICHAEL's eye*

MICHAEL

[to JACOB's hand, hurt]

You don't... remember?


*JACOB's eyes are busy, he's taking a moment to catch up, but he's found it*


JACOB

[quietly joyous]

Yeah, with the... 45 cent Olympic stamps

no, no, I do remember.

Of course, yeah.


*MICHAEL reaches a little, then retreats*


JACOB (ctnd.)

[genuine, light]

I'm sorry, it's...

it's nothing personal

I don't remember a lot from that time.

[trying to play it off]

trauma is a hell of a memory eraser.

*MICHAEL reaches all the way, taking JACOB's hand, it's encouraging without an ounce of pity*

MICHAEL

[deflating, sorry]

I'm sorry, I should've...

*JACOB smiles, it stops MICHAEL in his tracks*

MICHAEL

[trying to brush off]

...yeah, anyway. I just ask 'cause...

I treasured those letters

[changing, becoming sombre]

and, when... they stopped, I sort of

assumed the worst.

JACOB

[nodding]

Mmm, because of... yeah.

MICHAEL

[bashful, holding back]

And I... kept all your letters.


JACOB

[surprised, flattered]

You did?


MICHAEL

[still bashful, more comfortable]

...yeah. In a shoebox

that I covered in pictures

of bands from Abigail's

Dolly magazines


JACOB

[warm, smiling]

That's so cute.


MICHAEL

[confessing, loving]

Well, I wanted to hang onto you

I missed you so much

JACOB

[a little playful, loving]

You're very miss-able yourself

MICHAEL

[unsure, reaching]

Yeah?

JACOB

[affirming, loving]

Of course. I held onto you too.

**FADE OUT – Pink Wash**

**FADE OUT – Audio Track 2 – 'Radio'**

# Kent Music Report

# National Top 100 Singles

# Year End Chart

# 1987

# No.54

"Hey, I kinda didn't say something else before..." Jesse tries, self-inflicted-blame bubbling up from his stomach, lapping at his throat. "or, maybe it's a bit weird..."

"Like, weird how?" Matthew asks, with the tiniest dash of concern, which he then dismisses. "You know what, just say."

"I was... I mean, I feel bad about... not understanding what was going on with your dad, like not just after but at the time too, and..." Jesse elaborates, images of Peter's hateful, twisted, expression popping into his vision. "I don't know... trying to help more."

"What?" Matthew asks, bright yet confused, remembering Jesse's numerous defences. "You helped plenty!"

"I... did?" Jesse follows, trying to recall a moment he ever did enough.

"Yeah!" Matthew beams, warmth holding his heart, as the best days of his childhood surround him. "Being able to go over to your house was like... this refuge, this like... magical place... you were there... and we could go play at the park near your house, and your parents fed me the best food!"

Jesse watches with pleasant confusion, taking in the ray of light that is Matthew, as hands gesture happily, and lips and cheeks smile with every word.

Such an undimmable light, and here he is, sitting at the circle table in Jesse's apartment, in just briefs and a shirt, brighter than the beaming November spring sunshine, as it streams in, cupping him in it's warm hands.

"And sometimes... your sister would also play with us." Matthew continues, recalling Tabitha reading her Dolly magazines, and explaining her makeup supplies, with the pair watching on in awe. "It was... everything I needed."

He tries to piece it together, to hear Matthew genuinely, to reconcile the everyday moments, especially those where he acted less than favourable, and the reality his friend went back to.

But if Jesse wouldn't trade a second of those moments, maybe May wouldn't either.

"I guess I... I don't know, as an adult, I can see now what I truly couldn't wrap my head around then, and...

yeah." Jesse tries, wanting to hear Matthew's words, but something inside him pushing back against them. "But that's... really good to know."

"Yeah, it's good. It *was* good." Matthew replies, seeing Jesse disappear like before, offering a hand to the table. "But also, like, it wasn't all on you."

Fingers gliding over to Matthew, settling into an easy hold, a tether to the present, as his brain threatens to retreat to the past.

"And like I say, I had Mum, I had Daniel." Matthew continues, eyes on hands, feeling Jesse tremble ever so. "He would stand up for me like no one else, he was like... my protector at home."

"Ok. I guess I just... I dunno, wanted to take care of you better." Jesse confesses, before realising how he might sound, and rushing to clarify. "Not that... like, obviously your home life wasn't about me, like, I'm not trying to, like, say my feelings matter more, or-"

"Hey... hey, hey." Matthew interrupts, soft and loving, seeing the spiral loop behind walnut eyes. "I wasn't hearing that. And you did. Just by being my friend."

"Sorry, yeah... I dunno. I guess I want to..." Jesse mumbles, the hot wash of two-fold guilt rising up within him, wanting to retreat in every way. "...yeah, I just... I dunno."

"Who does?" Matthew asks lightly, squeezing gently, feeling the stillness in Jesse's fingertips. "Spending time with you and your family was more than enough."

"I wanted to give you more, though." Jesse spills, the sentiment coming out too quickly this time, unable to be censored or slowed. "I mean..."

How much clearer it all becomes instantly. This was never about a debt Jesse wanted to pay, but about a love he hadn't been able to share.

And the shaking, Jesse trying to pull back, and Matthew bringing up his other hand, catching those fingers.

"I won't let you." He promises, trying to catch low, brown eyes. "You need to keep some for yourself."

"I... do?" Jesse asks, looking up to loving, dark eyes.

"Yeah." Matthew affirms, low and warm. "And anyway, I can't hold it all, you gotta help me out, keep some for yourself."

A tiny, half-hearted, single chuckle floats out of Jesse.

"...yeah."

"Yeah."

Kent Music Report

National Top 100 Singles

Year End Chart

1979

No. 66

Hands exploring planes and ridges, soapy washcloths gliding over skin, occasional kisses, water cascading down and over, carving a path in it's wake.

Slow, gentle, soft.

Two people in a shared trance, communicating silently, moving together, no spot off limits.

Eyes taking in shoulders and nipples and belly buttons and hips and thighs. Gazes hungry and curious.

Seeing each other only after sex, backwards as queerness often is. Not able to follow the path set out, needing to forge it's own.

Bodies clean, towels on skin, not quite enough space for two in Jesse's bathroom.

But, in the closeness, a chance to finally pose a burning question.

"So... denial as well?" Matthew asks, towel-drying his hair, eyes on Jesse. "I was kind of winging it, so..."

"Yeah... yeah, for sure." Jesse agrees, slinging his towel over his shoulders, fingers holding each end. "You winged it well, if that's..."

"Yeah, that's... yeah." Matthew nods, drying his legs, eyes down.

"We didn't... like, about aftercare..." Jesse tries, fingers squeezing into the towel. "...did you...?"

"Uh, I guess, like, this is good." Matthew replies, a swift glance up, then returning to the bath mat. "Maybe some... laying down, in-in a bit."

"I like cuddling, and I don't- like, not that you are..." Jesse stumbles, gaze boring into the back of Matthew's head. "...but I don't attach any like... I mean, tops can like cuddling."

Matthew can feel it. A sharpness. Right between the scapulae. A shot to his spine.

"Nah yeah, sure sure, I didn't..." He mumbles, the words tumbling right from the darkest part of his brain, to his lips, before he catches himself. "I mean, I guess I did... a bit."

And the sharpness. Pulling out. A steak from his back. Freedom in the wound it left.

"Nice." Jesse breathes, relief softening his unseen intense stare. "I just... I mean, my undies were a mess, so like... shower first."

"Yeah, shower was nice." Matthew agrees, straightening up finally, unable to pretend his legs weren't dry any longer. "And I didn't mean I wanted you to be uncomfortable. I mean... unless you wanted to be."

Jesse considers for a moment, nothing surging into his mind in the haze of release without pleasure. It was the short-circuiting that he enjoyed, but in this case, it wasn't as welcomed.

"I'm sure we can come up with something." He concludes, leaning in enough for Matthew to close the gap.

"Absolutely."

Matthew glancing down to lips that taste of him, his hand lazily landing on the back of Jesse's neck, guiding closer.

Lips meeting softly, a little taste as they part, unmistakable and raw. Breathing in, sinking, pulling apart too soon.

"Well, shall we?" Jesse asks, nodding toward the door.

"Oh... yeah." Matthew realises, blinking back from his daze, remembering the offer to get into bed.

A towel hung up, another joining, a hand from the shoulder, to the elbow, to the wrist, and into the palm.

Jesse leading Matthew to his bed, barefoot treading softly on freshly vacuumed carpet, goosebumps popping up on bronze skin, a shiver snaking up his spine.

Shins brushing up against clean sheets, a hand falling from grasp, crawling up and inside, folding one side down for Matthew.

"So, yes to denial." He muses, turning to lay on his side, facing his guest. "It can be a little spur of the moment though."

"Oh?" Matthew replies, knee-first and palms on crisp, chalk white, sheets. "You wanna top your own denial from the bottom?"

".. I guess." Jesse considers, the thought never quite occurring to him in the past. "I mean, I'll ask, and... you could decide."

"Mmmm." Matthew hums, stretching legs out under the duvet, covering his naked body in its warmth. "Interesting."

"That sounds promising." Jesse encourages, looking over the man who had been so certain, suddenly dripping with a nervousness.

A stiff Matthew, staring up at the ceiling, now so shy, so uncertain, the intimacy hitting him after the moment, holding him down.

And, like a rescue mission, fingers walking over to him, spotted in his peripheral, sweet and slow and playful. Such a Jesse move.

He shifts just his head, watching the two fingers approach, leaving Jesse's skin, and travelling over one chalk white pillow, then another, and down towards his arm, finally reaching almond skin, touches so light he can barely feel them, and still he watches, completely entranced.

Jesse glancing from his fingers, to Matthew's face, and back, as he walks from upper arm, over the small drop, to pectoral, and down into the dip in Matthew's sternum.

Fingers fanning out, palm settling against ribcage, hand on heart.

"Is this okay?" He asks, eyes locked on Matthew's face.

Onyx eyes travelling from nails, to knuckles, then wrist, over forearm, up to elbow, around to shoulder, up the neck, across the chin, along lips, up to nose, and finally, meeting waiting, warm, walnut eyes.

"...yeah."

Beats against palm becoming slower, more even, settling into Jesse's bed, his touch, his space, watching him, being watched by him, locked into breathing, into touch, swimming through a moment together.

"...this is nice." Matthew says, bringing his palm up to cover Jesse's.

A small 'mmm' from Jesse as he glides his thumb up to Matthew's, tracing over the knuckle with such control and gentleness, it takes a beat to be noticed.

Matthew glancing down, watching the small movement for a breath, then circling his thumb around.

Jesse following, round and round, calm and tender, light enough to slow time, to sink into the moment, to feel the body settle absolutely and completely.

And it tumbles out, without even thinking.

"It's not usually like this for me." Matthew admits, looking back to Jesse, safe enough to speak freely. "It's not... yeah, just not like this."

"Do you... like this?" Jesse follows up, genuinely curious, not aiming to pry or feeling entitled to know, simply a desire to re-meet this man.

"...yeah."

It's small and honest, but it says everything it needs to.

Jesse hears the sex without intimacy, he sees the lack of aftercare, he feels the tension of the post-nut clarity in a strangers apartment.

"But it's not like... I mean, I'm not saying that, like..." Matthew tries, a pang of guilt stabbing him, suddenly hot under the lightweight duvet. "...not that, like... I mean, sometimes I do just want sex... and that's fine, that's not like, bad or something, it's something I enjoy, and like... urgh, I don't thin I'm getting this across."

"Some writer you are." Jesse jokes, pressing his palm against Matthew's heart. "But I get you."

"You do?"

"Yeah, like... I love hook-up apps, I love having sex with men, It's like..." Jesse elaborates, snapshots of nameless men of all shapes and sizes flashing in his mind, hands on his body, cocks and clits in his mouth, and cum on his lips. "I don't know, life-affirming and sort of... gender-affirming too, if that makes sense?"

"Perfect sense."

"Yeah, and it's like, sort of like, it'll be a good hook-up, it'll be hot and sweaty, and he'll do the things we discussed, and I'll do my things, and then..." Jesse continues, that all-too-familiar sinking feeling flooding his body as he recalls. "...it can feel a bit... hollow without... you know, like, after a while."

Matthew soaking Jesse's words in, allowing them to settle into his brain, and enter his bloodstream, and a deep breath fills his lungs, refreshing and true.

"...yeah."

A small, shared smile, an understanding, a collective experience despite so much time apart.

And Matthew's smile dampens as his writer's curiosity gets the better of him.

"Hey... can I... ask something, like, personal?" He asks, tracing his hand back just enough to interlace his fingers in Jesse's.

"Please do."

"Okay, so... when did you realise you liked boys?" Matthew asks, hoping it would come across as genuine interest and not orientation interrogation.

"Oh, I always knew I liked boys." Jesse shrugs, assuming it was as obvious to May as it had been to him.

"You did?" Matthew blurts, shifting under the duvet to turn onto his side and fully face Jesse.

"Yeah, of course." Jesse elaborates, watching Matthew shuffle and adjust, an unpredicted, but welcome response. "I liked you, I even kind of had a thing for Eric even though he was a dick. I liked-"

"Wait... Eric?" Matthew interrupts, trying to picture an 'Eric' they both knew.

"Like, from Primary School." Jesse explains, seeing the grating, but somewhat spunky, brown-haired white boy in his red and black uniform.

"Oh wow." Matthew muses, recalling a white face with freckles and cruel, blue eyes, and that laugh, that soul-cutting, mocking, laugh.

"Yeah, this goes way back. I always knew about boys." Jesse continues, numerous men on the TV swimming through his mind in an instant.

Watching rage on a weekend morning, seeing all the young men dancing and singing and playing instruments. All those US-exports plastered all over a small-town Australian screen, in glorious, terrestrial, 4:3 aspect ratio, and he, a young boy, not knowing what to do with his desire.

Thinking of wearing their clothes, licking their hair, drinking from the same cup, hoping to get a little bit of their saliva in his mouth. It was everything to a queer boy in Oberon to bare witness to all three members of blink-182 running around naked in the 'What's My Age Again?' video, and how it ran his mind rampant to wonder what it'd be like to see a naked man in real life.

"And then..." He continues, pushing the memories of stroking his cock to Nick Carter from his mind's eye. "I don't know, I guess my type of women is kind of specific, so... it took me longer to realise."

Matthew watching Jesse's face, seeing the man come and go, and trying to think if he'd ever been attracted to a woman, and what she might be like for him to feel that way.

"And what's your type of women?" He asks, mind flicking through musicians and actresses, hoping to find one he might remember being alluring.

"I mean…" Jesse begins, a few faces flashing up, before Clove's lingers, clear as day. "…not to sound like a fucking pain slut bottom, but… tops."

"And it's hard to find women who are tops?" Matthew rushes, finally realising the lead singer of Garbage did have him tingling more than once, then registering his words, and trying to salvage himself. "I don't mean to sound… it's just… I don't think about it much, so…"

"Nah, it's all good." Jesse affirms, eyes looking to Matthew, but mind seeing Clove. "It can be hard, cause like… society tells women to be like… small and agreeable, so finding one who has sort of actively strayed from that is sort of like-"

"Finding a man who isn't hung up on cuddling." Matthew rushes in, smile on blush lips.

"I mean…" Jesse agrees, raising his eyebrows, Matthew coming into focus.

"Mmm."

# XO by American Rock Band

# Fall Out Boy

Powerful hips working feverishly, grinding onto Jesse's cock, surrounding and engulfing him completely, as all Jesse can do is watch.

Matthew's hands gripping just above his knees, squeezing into the soft flesh, pinning his legs down, as hips hold hips, and rope holds wrists.

Looking over Matthew's form, marvelling at the man taking him, riding him, controlling him absolutely. Eyes moving from strong thighs, to bucking hips, from bouncing, hard, cock, up to winding torso, and flushed chest, cheeks, and lips, to jet black, dead straight hair, falling over onyx, watchful, gaze.

The most magnificent sight in this, or any, universe, Jesse can barely believe his eyes, let alone take in the hip-shaking sensation that is his slick cock, grinding against the hot walls of Matthew's pulsing arse.

Matthew feeling his walls gripping, his untouched cock pulsing, watching an enamoured Jesse, under streams of February sun peaking through curtains.

Palms red against ropes, arms stretched, bronze skin blushing under sporadic tatts, chest heaving with every buck, wanton, walnut eyes on Matthew, fiery intensity burning strong.

What incredible beauty, to feel such pleasure, and see intense pleasure reflected back. Two notes, creating the shortest, yet strongest, and most harmonious, chord.

Matthew pausing, holding them both for a moment, a breath from release.

"Are you gonna cum for me?" He asks, tracing one hand back towards himself, pausing for a moment on his own thigh.

"Y-yes... I... yes..." Jesse blurts, eyes fixed on Matthew's hand.

A smile, a glimmer in the gaze, a slow circle of the hips.

"Mmm?" Matthew teases, tracing fingertips up to his cock, feeling and seeing a twitch, giving himself away just enough.

"Yes... pl-please..." Jesse begs, unable to focus on either face or hips, and darting back and forth feverishly.

"Please?" Matthew grins, fingers gliding up his shaft, delighting in the delicious sounds falling from salmon lips.

"Mhmm... please, May..." Jesse pleads, face as red as his palms, wanting against anything to thrust up, he's almost there.

"Oh, 'May' now?" Matthew replies, a moan escaping his lips as he circles the wet spot on his tip, boring intense eyes into Jesse's pleading gaze.

"Or... M-Matthew?" Jesse stumbles, watching enviously as Matthew strokes slowly.

"Mmm... both are..." Matthew begins, hitching his hips up just a little. "Fine." His final word punctuated with a quick drop down.

Jesse moans into the room, straining against his ropes, cock twitching inside Matthew, catching a glimpse of the devilish smile before his eyes slam shut.

For a beat he's floating, body so tense yet mind so focused, a heightened Zen state he's enjoyed many times before. He doesn't want it to end, yet can't help but reach for that final throw that would really send him over the edge.

Eyes open, Matthew's cheeky grin greeting him, one hand on cock, walls fluttering around his own, the other hand pressing into his thigh so hard, he's already relishing the bruise.

"Ready?" Matthew asks, speeding his strokes. "You gonna be a good boy for me?"

The trigger phrase almost sends Matthew himself into ecstasy, his cock stroking, Jesse's twitching cock inside him, watching his words affect Jesse like this, while a breath away from rhapsody, it's a wonder he isn't spilling out already.

Jesse can only moan in response, mouth falling open, eyes on Matthew's cock, hoping his request is clear.

"You want it there?" Matthew teases, aiming his cock, slow circles resuming.

A nod in response. Jesse too far gone to manage words, hands in fists, thighs tense, orgasm right there.

A smile as reply. Matthew relishing in the effect he has on Jesse, and the glorious mix of dominance and submission he's embodying.

Fast and fierce, Matthew is grinding, stroking, aiming, feeling it build again, relief in the sensation, lost in the absolute bliss.

Onyx eyes on Jesse, watching himself be watched, feeling another twitch, hearing the gorgeous sounds of pleasure escape those suddenly plump, salmon, lips. Nearly.

It's there, right there, he can feel it, threatening to rush through his system like lightening.

A buck from Jesse, unexpected and intense, and he's flying. Spilling onto Jesse's chest, a few drops making it to plump lips and blushing cheeks. His walls pulsing, the dual sensation shaking his legs, cascading deep moans through his chest and out his lips, throwing his head to the ceiling, arching his back, as waves and waves rush around his body, alighting every nerve, tingling every cell. Falling into a fold in time, body feeling more than he thought possible, eyes slamming shut in the intense beauty of release and pulses, like he is the Ying and Yang at once.

Jesse tasting, licking, watching, enraptured in the sight of Matthew. Chin up, hair cascading back, Adam's Apple rising and falling, skin flushed like never before, deep carmine shining through almond tones, back arching, accentuating that body lewdly, gloriously, a snapshot of absolute sexuality.

Matthew pulsing around his cock, and the taste of cum on his lips, Jesse thrusts up again, and one twitch, two, his whole body tenses, shuddering under utter sublimity, the orgasm roaring through him, electricity ravaging up and down his spine, cock spilling into a shaking Matthew, twitching in time with pulses, the planets lining up, sacred blessings running from one, to the other, and back again.

Beautiful sounds falling from both of them, sensation bubbling over into heaves, moans, and whimpers, exchanging of ecstasy back and forth.

Feeling the white-hot burst inside, sending Matthew to another release, deep inside him, like he's riding on absolute elation within his very soul, hand off his all-too-sensitive cock, and gripping tightly into Jesse's side, fingers sinking just below the ribs, holding on for dear life.

Jesse feeling the second orgasm as much as seeing it, the hot walls grabbing him, milking more out of his twitching cock, Matthew's hands all over him, the thighs wrapped around him, completely held and taken, like seeing a truth in Matthew no one else gets to see.

Ravaging, deep sounds, tumbling out of Matthew, body seizing around Jesse, cock hitting just the right spot, feeling and hearing the satisfaction beneath him, as over and over the sensation rides through his body, taking him somewhere he's never been.

Sacred and secret, Jesse's moans cool to shaky breaths, and finally, to sighs of satisfaction, as he feels himself tumble back to Earth, grounded and surrounded, as he loves to be.

Matthew taking another moment, the release only shuddering to a dull gradually, as he starts to feel his unsteady, spent thighs, his tingly, tired hands, his ragged, uneven breath.

One last aftershock shaking Matthew, eyes widening, breath hitching, a moment taken to steady himself.

And laughter, thick and rich like caramel, spreading to Jesse with ease.

Matthew loosening his grip, placing his hands either side of Jesse, and pushing himself up just enough to ease off a half-soft cock, as it unceremoniously flops to Jesse's stomach.

Another laugh, quickly becoming a 'ow' as Matthew feels just how much he's worked his legs, a concerned look from Jesse, his gaze moving from his own floppy cock to Matthew's contorted face.

"You ok?" He asks, looking up with sudden concern.

"Shouldn't I be asking you that?" Matthew jokes, flopping to the side. "You're the one who's tied up, after all."

A small chuckle as Matthew reaches for the rope, propping himself up on his side, pulling the knot free with one yank, and looking over Jesse's satiated body. Droplets of cum drying all over his chest and chin, skin glistening with sweat, serene look on his face, truly a sight to behold.

"Hey come on now!" Jesse protests, wincing as he pulls his arms down. "Let's not buy into the 'only the sub needs aftercare' business."

"Nah, nah, you're right for sure." Matthew concedes, tracing a circle around one of the droplets on Jesse's chest.

"And you still didn't answer my question." Jesse reiterates, bringing a red palm up to cup Matthew's face. "You ok?"

His expression so soft, looking up into such dark eyes, lost in the cosmos again, wanting only to check in with an old friend.

'Nah yeah I'm good." Matthew smiles, eyes glancing to Jesse's lips. "Just my legs were ragged. A kiss would help, but."

"Oh it would now?" Jesse jokes, propping up, bridging the gap halfway.

"Yeah, it would." Matthew volleys, eyes closing, leaning in.

Lips meeting lips and tongues on tongues as the last ounce of sexual energy is exchanged back and forth, hands coming up to faces, pulling in deeper, thighs on thighs, then chest on chest and hips flush as Jesse climbs up to feel Matthew's body completely.

Busy hands move from shoulders, down Jesse's back, to that ample arse, sinking hungry fingers into soft flesh, pulling closer still, hot, glistening, skin so close, release still floating around, barely gone from their systems.

Excerpt from:

# MY HAND

# IN YOURS

Written & Directed

By

Matthew Seng

# SCENE SIXTEEN
# HAPPILY EVER AFTER

**lounge room, sofa, armchair, coffee table**
**all pushed back to upstage left centre**

*JACOB and MICHAEL are slow dancing together*

*There's an ease in the way they move, it's calming,*
*yet charged with romance and sex*

**FADE UP – Pink Wash**

**FADE UP – Audio Track 8 – 'Come Away With Me**
**– Norah Jones'**

*JACOB twirls MICHAEL out, and back in, both facing*
*audience, swaying back and forth, eyes closed*

**FADE DOWN, HALF VOLUME – Audio Track 8 –**
**'Come Away With Me – Norah Jones'**

MICHAEL

[half-joking, with love]

So is this too cheesy?

Too 'happily ever after' for you?


*JACOB smiles, The smile goes unseen by MICHAEL*


JACOB

[half-joking, wistful]

I can do a little cheesy.

I do have a heart.


MICHAEL

[content]

Yeah, I know...

I can feel it.


JACOB

[content]

It's not giving me away, is it?

MICHAEL

[a little playful]

Not really.

Further down, though…


*MICHAEL pushes his hips back*


*JACOB hunches at the sensation. Reminded of his own arousal suddenly*


JACOB

[affectionately]

You little shit.


*MICHAEL moves to face JACOB.*


*MICHAEL and JACOB are side-on to the audience*


*JACOB is playfully appalled*


*MICHAEL tries to lean in*


*JACOB pulls back teasingly*

*A short beat. JACOB AND MICHAEL look over each other hungrily*

*JACOB pulls MICHAEL in for a kiss. It's short, real, and passionate*

*JACOB pulls back, smiling devilishly*

*MICHAEL exhales with sexual charge, he wants more yet loves following JACOB's lead*

*JACOB takes in the sight of MICHAEL, biting his lip. JACOB pulls MICHAEL back into waltzing*

MICHAEL

[sexually charged]

You're terrible.

JACOB

[teasing, sexual]

And you fucking love it.

MICHAEL

[calmer, still sexually charged]

I do. You know me too well.


*JACOB and MICHAEL laugh, softly, calming both,*
*falling back into slow dancing*


MICHAEL (ctnd.)

[calmer, content]

…I like this.


JACOB

[content]

…me too. I like it, too.


*MICHAEL turns in JACOB's arms, facing JACOB,*
*placing a hand on JACOB's cheek*


MICHAEL

[content]

look at you…

JACOB

[half-joking, still content]

…you are.

[genuine]

What do you think?


MICHAEL

[half-joking]

Pretty good.

MICHAEL (ctnd.)

[short pause, considering]

…really good…


JACOB

[half-joking, still content]

…yeah?


MICHAEL

[half-joking]

Of course.


*JACOB smiles, it's incredibly warm, unwaveringly
genuine, he is enraptured by MICHAEL*

*MICHAEL smiles back, with the exact same warmth and genuineness*

*JACOB leans in for a kiss, slowly, it takes a short moment. And it's worth it*

*MICHAEL and JACOB kiss. Chaste, short, and sweet*

*JACOB pulling back first, hand on MICHAEL's lower back, dipping MICHAEL*

*MICHAEL following without hesitation, head back, completely trusting in JACOB, his leg coming up, knee to JACOB's hip*

*The pair pause in an impossibly low dip for a beat, it's sensual, sexual, JACOB watching MICHAEL enjoy it all*

*JACOB guides MICHAEL back up, it's slow yet strong, and JACOB pulls MICHAEL in impossibly close, lips brushing*

MICHAEL

[flirting]

Oh… what's this?


JACOB

[leading, flirting]

What do you want it to be?


MICHAEL

[genuine, loving]

…anything.


*JACOB pulls MICHAEL into a powerful kiss, it's passionate and sexual, hands everywhere, bodies close*


**FADE OUT – Pink Wash**

**FADE OUT – Audio Track 8 – 'Come Away With Me – Norah Jones'**

# Dear Reader,

Thank you for purchasing and reading 'We Used To Hold Hands All The Time', and, as usual, if you're skipping to the end, please go back and read the story first.

We can never experience stories for the first time again, so savour the chance to dive in not knowing where you're going.

So, you've finished the story of Matthew and Jesse, two layered, vibrant, characters I love very dearly.

Hopefully you saw yourself in these two, felt their pains and triumphs, and lived a little bit of their lives by spending this time with them.

I said 'no Happy Endings', but maybe I lied. Or maybe not.

My aim as a writer isn't to create a plot, or give a clear beginning, middle, and end. It's to allow you, The Reader, to peak into moments in someone's life. And then stand back, piece it all together, and see an entire picture.

Memories are funny that way, they don't always come back to me correctly, or in order. So I aim to create a similarly disorienting sensation.

If you've followed me online, you'll know this one came out like a kidney stone, and I'm relieved to be finished with it. But very scared it won't live up to the wait.

Hopefully you'll let me know.

Either way, thank you for allowing me, Jesse, and Matthew into your life. I hope you enjoyed the journey. I appreciate my words being a part of yours.

Kind regards,
Neptune Henriksen

# About The Author

Neptune Henriksen is a critically acclaimed writer and theatre maker, as well as an award-winning director.

Their works explore identity, sexuality, and emotional turmoil through a queer, intersectional lens, with love, humour, and introspection.

Their art is prolific and varied, from storytelling to comedy directing, microfiction to physical theatre, with their artistic voice always shining through, unique and clear.

Their works seek to comfort, to explore, and to shed light on topics often shied away from.

# Other Works By The Author

## Queer Summer Trilogy, 2022-2023

Three novellas of queer romance in the Australian Summer.
1. 'Where The Pink Meets The Blue', a bisexual erotica
2. 'Under A Summer Sky In January', a sapphic teen love triangle
3. 'We Used To Hold Hands All The Time', A romance of childhood friends reunited

## 'Daydreamings: A Collection Of Connections', 2020

A flash fiction collection, snapshots of moments of connection and relationships of all intersections.